THE MILFORD SERIES

Popular Writers of Today

VOLUME TEN

The Delany Intersection

Samuel R. Delany

Considered As a Writer of
Semi-Precious Words

George Edgar Slusser

R. REGINALD
THE Borgo Press
SAN BERNARDINO, CALIFORNIA
MCMLXXVII

For Steve and Roberta—
"Beyond the vale of mist and clouds."

Library of Congress Cataloging in Publication Data:

Slusser, George Edgar.
The Delany intersection.

(Popular writers of today; v. 10) (The Milford series)
Bibliography: p. 64.
1. Delany, Samuel R.—Criticism and interpretation. I. Title.
PS3554.E437Z9 813′.5′4 77-24580
ISBN 0-89370-214-5

Produced, designed, and published by R. Reginald, The Borgo Press, P.O. Box 2845, San Bernardino, CA 92406. Composition by Mary A. Burgess. Cover design by Judy Cloyd. Printed in the United States of America by Griffin Printing and Lithography Co., Inc., Glendale, CA.

First Edition———December, 1977

THE DELANY INTERSECTIONS

The fiction of Samuel R. Delany seems a striking example of what Robert Scholes calls the "structuralist imagination." This fancy phrase describes an approach to literary creation which is essentially post-mimetic in nature. Instead of reflecting some objective "reality," the fictional work is seen as primarily a word-construct, a self-contained system whose relation to our familiar world is homologous, but in no way necessary or determined by it. Both in theory and in practice, Delany's "speculative fiction" (SF) is structuralist. Delany is a rare combination of imaginative writer and articulate critic. Because both of these operations are informed by the same imagination, they are reflexive, mutually illuminating. In fact, probably the best way to understand the complex functioning of these novels is to examine the same processes at work in his critical utterances. Delany's essays, of course, are important in their own right as well, for they expand the traditional vistas of science fiction considerably. If extrapolation is to become what Delany calls speculation, there must be awareness of the dual role of language in this world-building process. Words have the power both to create new worlds, and at the same time to make the reader aware of the "structure" or system that underlies the process of construction. To Delany writing an SF novel is a verbal activity that is simultaneously visionary and analytical. In this sense, his claims (and his works) are far-reaching and revolutionary. Indeed, he turns the tables on the defenders of the "mainstream," for he sees his chosen (and much maligned) genre as the one, among all modern forms, most supremely suited to this structuralist task.

For Delany, as for the structuralist critics, literary creation is essentially linguistic activity, what Roland Barthes describes in broad terms as "the strictly human process by which men give meaning to things." At the base of Delany's comments on the nature and role of fiction is the seminal perception of Saussurian linguistics—that the relationship between word and object is arbitrary, neither determined nor fixed. This idea has had a great impact, both on the study of myth, and on that of literature. On one hand, it suspends the hegemony of primitivism; on the other, that of realism. In a recent article entitled "The Profession of Science Fiction: VIII: Shadows—Part Two" (*Foundation* 7 & 8, 1975), Delany cites an epigram of Levi-Strauss, the structuralist anthropologist: "Music and mythology confront man with virtual objects whose shadow alone is real." The process of mythmaking is turned around here. The "virtuality" of myth shifts the emphasis from cause to effect; what is substantial is not an "object" but its various projections in time and space. Delany's work is full of both music and myth.

That he sees such "shadows" as essentially verbal constructs is clear. Here is his definition of SF from the same essay: "Science fiction is a way of casting a language shadow over coherent areas of imagination-space that would otherwise be largely inaccessible." These "shadows" are what Barthes calls *similacra*—the "real" is decomposed and recomposed so that between "the two tenses of structuralist activity" (word and object) something new emerges. What is new is "intelligibility." The goal of such activity, says Barthes, "whether reflexive or poetic, is to reconstruct an 'object' in such a way as to manifest thereby the rules of functioning of this object." In Delany's fiction, creation is simultaneously reflexive and poetic, projective and critical. This essay will trace the workings of this process in his major novels.

In another article, "About Five Thousand Seven Hundred and Fifty Words" (*Science Fiction Review* 33, October 1969), Delany makes a distinction between SF and what he calls, respectively, "naturalistic fiction" and "fantasy." This distinction is drawn in terms that are primarily linguistic (and structuralist), and repays close attention. What differentiates these two modes of fiction is not "truth to life"—which implies some absolute and determined relationship between external "reality" and words—but what Delany calls their "level of subjunctivity": "Subjunctivity is the tension on the thread of meaning that runs between word and object." The various forms are described as inflexions in tense and mood: in fantasy the events "could not have happened"; in naturalistic fiction they "could have happened"; SF is distinguished from these by the fact that events here simply "have not happened." Whatever the adequacy of this schema, the pattern it inscribes is clear. Its implications, in fact, are diachronic as well as synchronic. The two dominant fictional forms of the 19th century are defined by the logical opposition "could/could not." Contained in the modal auxiliary is an inflexion toward prescription: the deadlock ultimately becomes a matter of entrenched opinion. The way to break this is to see the relationship of these two terms differently: not as an either-or situation, but as a process of interaction. Indeed, much of the difficulty in understanding certain "problem" works of the 19th century may come from this refusal to see the conflict of "genres" as other than irreconcilable. Take Flaubert's *Salammbo*. On one hand, the author seeks, through laborious archeological research, to reconstruct Carthage, thus showing that the struggles of his characters could have happened. On the other, his ornate, fantastic style gives us just the opposite impression: it could not have happened as told. But does grasping a novel like this on the neutral level of system make it speculative fiction? Delany subdivides SF, one of his sub-categories is the parallel world story—events that "have not happened in the past." Suddenly another opposition forms, this time on the descriptive plane, but bringing tension nonetheless. In passing, Delany had described a third mode of fiction, "reportage," in which events "happened." All at once, this becomes important; to what extent have the events in *Salammbo* happened, or those in Dick's *Man in the High Castle* not happened? System generates system. Like his fiction, Delany's critical visions are protean—balances are constantly forming and breaking down. Here there is, literally, a dance of unstable patterns: twos, threes, even fours. How do we arrange these elements? Fantasy is to naturalism as reportage is to SF. Or is it rather: Fantasy is to SF as reportage is to naturalism? In either case we cancel out fantasy, and naturalism to emerge with a significantly modern dichotomy. At one extreme, verbal activity is focused on *what* is meant (the *signifie*); at the other, *how* it is meant, (the *signifiant* or structure). There is either no novel, or (to use Delany's word) the "multiplex" novel. SF, then, is not a byway of modern literature, but its mainstream.

Delany has made interesting conjectures not only on the nature of SF but on its origins as well. One of the most intriguing is the possibility of a relationship between American SF and French symbolism. There are, of course, real affinities between symbolism and Delany's structuralist idea of SF (Barthes's statement that "discourse is not simply an adding together of sentences: it is, itself, one great sentence" shows that the same current nourishes both). More than this, there is perhaps a direct symbolist influence on Delany himself. There are many different symbolist "activities"; but the strain that leads from Rimbaud to the surrealists seems most fascinating to Delany. Instead of the vertical correspondances of Mallarme, he prefers the horizontal displacements practiced by Rimbaud—synaesthesia and the poetry of prose. Rimbaud is everywhere in his work: from Rydra Wong's starship to Tak Loufer's bookshelf, from the fascination with criminal artists to the *saisons en enfer* of *The Tides of Lust* and *Dhalgren*. The current runs much deeper than allusions and themes, however. In Delany's eyes, SF is an eminently mystical mode of literature—this is the natural outgrowth of speculation on man's place in the universe. As a writer, though, Delany is less interested in deciphering some Great Book or *grimoire* than (to use his words) in projecting a "feel" of the mystical—creating those moments when the pressure of reason "tends to squeeze all mysticism into one bright chunk that blurs all resolutions." To do this he follows Rimbaud's *voyant* in seeking to produce (again Delany's words) a "resonant aesthetic form." Implied in Rimbaud's *dereglement raisonne des sens* is simultaneous immersion and detachment, creation at the level of system. Rimbaud could then stand as ancestor to the sort of verbal activity (at once mystical and self-consciously analytical) that Delany prescribes for SF. For Delany, as for Rimbaud, the writer is, at one and the same time, the demiurgic creator of word-worlds, and their dispassionate explorer.

In his essay "Critical Methods: Speculative Fiction" (*Quark*/1, 1970), Delany offers in place of what he calls the "Victorian" idea of progress—the historical positivism that dominated the early "SF" of Wells and Verne—his more flexible "model" for constructing fictional worlds, in which (as in de Saussure's concept of language itself) there is no progress, only change. According to this model, at any stage of development all elements are present; only their function is different. What remains to be described is Delany's basic structure—those elements or patterns which, present on all levels of his text, combine to generate his larger forms. The best way to do this, perhaps, is to compare Delany's "world" with those of two other American writers of SF frequently mentioned by him—Heinlein and Le Guin. The fact that all these writers are American is important. Heinlein is a "primitive" writer, Le Guin is highly literate. And yet both, apparently, are in the sway of those "transcendentalist" patterns (the native blending of fundamental religion with that same Romantic nature philosophy that in France gave rise to symbolism) which have deterred many American writers from the Wellsian vision. Heinlein preaches progress, but does not practice it; Le Guin ironically undercuts it. The science fiction of both, however, like that of Delany, is the product of the same world view—one that accords marvelously with structuralism.

Though Heinlein constantly tells us his universe has *telos*, in reality it is static. In fact, his strongly Calvinist vision has shaped his "future history" into a string of *exempla* which follow the same basic pattern—election. Both history and evolution are overridden and obviated by some predestined plan, by suspending acts of grace. In terms of Jakobsen's distinction between metaphoric and metonymic patterns, Heinlein's stories and novels are purest metaphor. Each one of them, as the contingencies of time and space fall away, mirror by analogy the same basic polarity—chosen man and revealed plan. In Heinlein, then, there is neither progress nor change. Le Guin's universe, like Delany's, is based upon the rhythms of change in permanence. There is, however, a difference in the ways these function in the two writers; it is subtle and yet significant. Le Guin's fictions are constructed of the same sort of ironic shifts Delany describes in his *Quark* article: "Technology has always run in both constructive and destructive directions at once. While Rome's engineers built amazing stone aqueducts with engineering techniques that astound us today, her aristocracy was unintentionally committing mass suicide with lead-based cosmetics and lead-lined wine jars." Generally, though, in the patterning of Le Guin's universe, these cusps function in a rather abstract manner, paradoxes that illustrate both the complexity and the order of change. If individual human acts go awry, the system remains, and balance is invariably established. Though Le Guin's system is much more amenable to man, its symmetry is every bit as perfect as that which underlies Harlan Ellison's "The Beast That Shouted Love at the Heart of the World." Indeed, if man in Le Guin does not progress, he nevertheless has a history. Her Hainish world does not evolve in linear fashion. Yet out of the constant criss-crossing back and forth in time and space grows first a fabric, then a chronology. The poles may be fixed, but there is incessant movement between. In Le Guin's fiction, in a sense, metonymic displacement is subsumed in metaphoric analogy. Each world she creates is contiguous, displaced, and at the same time analagous, a mirror of change in permanence.

At a glance, Delany's fictional universe is similar and yet different. First, there is neither history nor cycle here. Each world creation is unique and self-contained. The relation between them, such as it exists, is more a lateral one of association and displacement than a vertical one of analogy. Further, the interior of each world is substantially different, marked by instability, metamorphosis, and permanent change rather than change in permanence. Delany's work may seem, at first, highly stylized or lushly ornate. This rigidity is merely a facade. All the various verbal screens,the disquisitions on symbolic logic, blend into a basic weave of imagery that is far more dynamic than static. Talk of paradox resolves into paradoxes, these in turn decomposing in ceaseless patterns of thrust and counterthrust. The dynamic nature of Delany's fiction comes from the fact that its central rhythm is not (as with Le Guin) binary alone, but rather continuous shifting between binary and ternary combinations, odds and evens. On all levels it is a fiction of unstable twos and broken threes: one boot, one bare foot, Prince Red's missing socket. Central to this process of change is the pivotal figure of the "intersection"—the point at which some duality, irreconcilable and unstable, intersects with a third term that suspends it. Here, as on a palimpsest (another favorite Delany image), double and triple rhythms are momentarily superimposed. Each of Delany's major novels has its intersection: Babel-17,Goedel's Law, metalogic.

A striking example of intersection—and one which preoccupied Delany the critic long before he incorporated it into the heart of his latest novel, *Triton*—is that of utopia and "heterotopia": Michel Foucault's "other place," the "shattering" of syntax and fable, the dissolving of the cement that holds the fabric of the known world—words and things—together. In his *Quark* article, "Critical Methods," Delany ponders the "irreconcilable utopian/dystopian conflict." Here again is a quandary with a diachronic locus: its "Wellsian parameters" must be suspended. Borrowing his terms from Auden, Delany does so by envisioning the utopian problem as a system rather than a conflict: "In the most truly Utopian of New Jerusalems, sometime you will find yourself in front of an innocuous-looking door; go through it, and you will find yourself, aghast, before some remnant of the Land of the Flies; in the most dehumanized Brave New World, one evening as you wander through the dreary public park, sunset bronzing the leaves will momentarily usher you into the most marvelous autumn evening in Arcadia. Similarly, in either Arcadia or the Land of the Flies, plans can be begun for either Brave New World or New Jerusalem." In this displacement, previous limits of vision ("you say it's good, I say it's bad") are suspended. Asimov's *Foundation* trilogy is neither utopian nor dystopian: "Its theme is the way in which a series of interrelated societies, over a historical period, force each other at different times back and forth from Utopian to Dystopian phases." The leap here is both a logical and an aesthetic one: "And whole new systems and syndromes of behavior. . . emerge." At this intersection the triad immediately modulates into a new binary combination—order and chaos. Douglas Barbour isolates the following phrase from Delany's first novel, *The Jewels of Aptor*: "Chaos caught in order, order defining chaos." Even the dynamics of Delany's latest novel, *Triton*, are bound up in a similar chiasmus, in which stability encompasses and nurtures the seed of new instability. Within the circle of nouns there is still the dynamic displacement of verbs "caught," "defining," the asymmetry of tenses. We are reminded of the poetry of e. e. cummings here, of a sonnet like the one that begins and ends on the phrase "conceive a man." This poem is simultaneously closed and open—there are neither capital letters nor periods to block the flow. We plunge into the middle of a laterally moving form. It ends at the beginning, and yet in the process of getting there, both "conceive" and "man" have changed meaning: instead of an intellectual construct, we have its opposite, a creation of nature. There is the same subtle and dynamic interplay of twos and threes here as in Delany. For this latter too, the chaos which opens is not that which closes the circle; and yet it is. Pivoting on this ambiguity, the triad holds—there is a beginning, middle and end—and at the same time dissolves back to the binary: change and permanence. This eccentric perpetual motion characterizes Delany's work in general.

The comparison with poetry is not fortuitous, for Delany himself sees SF as a mode of writing more akin to poetry than to the traditional realist novel. Each separate word for Delany, as for the symbolists he admires, is precious, the key to some magic world, and a value to be regenerated as it passes through new and more visionary word-systems. But there is a danger to such world-making as well—preciosity. In his *Quark* article, Delany makes SF comparable to poetry in its concern with "thingness." The "things" of science fiction, in America at least, are words: "The new American SF took on the practically incantatory task of naming nonexistant objects, then investing them with reality by a host of methods, technological and pseudo-technological explanations. . . or just inculcating them by pure repetition." However necessary this first step, Delany in 1970 sees it as "primitive—the incantatory word has become the visionary system. Yet at this level an even greater risk of preciosity appears. For if the structuralist activity is to be (as Barthes claims) a "human" one, there cannot be preoccupation with the *signifiant* to the exclusion of the *signifie*, with the synchronic to the exclusion of the diachronic, or, most importantly, with the freedom of relativity to the exclusion of a human constant defined by its limits. Delany's early novels may rely heavily on incantation. The later works, however, show that, if Delany twice felt the temptation of preciosity—his 1970 essay contains praise for Huysman's novel *A Rebours*, where symbolism lapses into decadence—twice he retreated from it to a position of balance and strength. His best novels (to use his own phrase) are rather "semi-precious" works. This term is not derogatory; on the contrary, it describes the poet's necessary coming to terms with the prose forms bequeathed to him by the narrative tradition in which he has chosen to work. Successively, Delany has turned to two major modes of prose fiction. First, in a series of adventures in time and space culminating in *Nova* (1968), he embraces the heroic epic. Then, after a period of experimentation which may in the long run prove to be transitional, he turns this basic pattern of the quest in the opposite direction, inward rather than out. If the conventional patterns upon which *Nova* is built are those of initiation and adventure, *Triton* (1976) works upon a different base—that of psychological fiction. Pivoting around these two novels, this study examines Delany's fiction at still a different intersection: the point where freedom to deconstruct and reconstruct worlds and the abiding conventional patterns—the narrative of deeds and the narrative of motives—meet and interact.

The novels in this *Nova* "cycle" are especially preoccupied with myth. Delany's approach to myth also has a tendency to "run in both constructive and destructive directions at once." This ambiguity and tension is built into the modern view of myth itself. Writers like Joseph Campbell and Northrop Frye, on one hand, believe that basic to all human endeavor and all literary genres alike is the myth of the quest—the endless search for meaning in human existence. On the other side, they state that no specific cultural variation of this "monomyth" is binding—these patterns describe, but do not prescribe, human behavior. In no way, then, is a man fated to relive any given mythic paradigm, or to follow any archetypal literary pattern. And yet somehow, if that man is to remain human, and recognizable as a hero, he is obliged to relive them. Contrary to what it may seem, Delany's universe remains a human one. True, Delany has a fascination with cyborgs, catmen, and other para-human forms. Yet there is far more here than what some have seen—a cosmic freak-show. If we look closely, we see that, beneath this surface, the human form divine tenaciously resists—just as at the center of these cultural explosions that lead to the wildest, most far-flung galactic civilizations our own twentieth century earth remains the key. Once again, this relationship between human and non-human, man and system, functions as a dynamic series of displacements and balances. Thus the dehumanization of the human form has its counterthrust—the humanization of technology, the "sockets" of *Nova*. Delany's novels of epic quest, especially *The Einstein Intersection* and *Nova*, will be studied in terms of this intersection of polymyth and monomyth.

The glories and perils of Delany's fictional approach to myth is mirrored in the work of a number of other American writers. Indeed, Delany himelf, in his *Quark* article, recognizes the problems that beset speculative world-making "in a country itself a potpourri of different cultural behavior patterns." Again a comparison may be found in the work of a poet, this time Gregory Corso, whom Delany quotes on the subject of myth in an epigraph to a chapter in *The Einstein Intersection*. In Corso's poem "Marriage," we witness a fascinating process—cultural myths are deconstructed and reconstructed. Here is what the speaker, with mock-epic bravado, would give to his dream-child: "For a rattle a bag of broken Bach records/Tack Della Francesca all over its crib/Sew the Greek alphabet on its bib/And build for its playpen a roofless Parthenon." This process is both valid and moving in this poem because it is rooted in the concrete yearnings of this pathetic seeker, whose own quest ("should I get married") echoes back in a series of mirror images, through "*She* in her lovely alien gaud waiting her Egyptian lover" (hinting at Keats's Ruth in her alien corn) back to the monomyth: the speaker's "activity" is grounded here. In Corso's later poems, however, cluttered with self-conscious allusions, we see the obverse of such *bricolage*—disembodied constructs, mythical bric-a-brac. Delany's evolution is quite different. After the early *The Fall of the Towers* (1961-64)—which is perhaps his high point of preciosity in this first cycle—there is gradual retreat toward the marvelous balance-in-tension of *Nova*. In this novel Delany comes close to fulfilling his own program, for the "shadows" of myth cast are somehow both virtual and real.

This study considers Delany's next two works, *The Tides of Lust* (1973) and *Dhalgren* (1975), as essentially transitional, elaborate fictional experiments that lead the author in a new fictional direction. If this study does not do justice to *Dhalgren*, it is because it cannot. Delany's interesting and provocative work is simply too complex to be dealt with in the short space this format allots. These two novels are in no way anomalies in Delany's career, surreal visions abandoned as the author returns to his true home in space in *Triton*. What is explored in these two novels is less the relation of questing man to myth than the relation of myth to the collective mind. This preoccupation is summarized in the statement (central to *Tides*) that man today has confused Faust and the Devil. From here it is only one step to exploration of a new relation—myth and the inner mind, the quest within of *Triton* (1976).

Scholes rightly distinguishes what he calls the "structualist novel" from its rival existentialist form in modern fiction. In this latter type, man is aware he is "engaged" in the process of history, and yet remains free to embrace his destiny, and in this limited sense to "make" it. Structuralist fiction, on the other hand, sets forth a system of forces whose center is not necessarily man and his existential problems—a world indifferent to his anxieties. What then is *Triton*? In one sense, it reads like an elaborate refutation of the existential novel, where even personal 'bravery' becomes little more than a subjective possibility constantly placed at the intersection with some other, indifferent system of logic. *Triton* also recreates the patterns of traditional psychological fiction, and not just to parody its hero's self-searchings. This is not a case of one form distorting an older one to overthrow it, or render it obsolete. On the contrary, we have intersection, an attempt to build a new mode of fiction upon this tension between two systems of narrative logic—the traditional *fabula* and its suspension in chaos. Delany has said that the speculative writer should explore, not condemn or condone. In his treatment of the "hero" of *Triton*, however, he is brought to do both. Here as in *Nova* he is clearly aiming at creation on the level of system. And yet the very nature of the convention chosen makes this stance more difficult. Tension in this novel approaches the breaking point.

Overriding the epic quest without and that within is something more central to Delany's world creation—its broader social fabric, what we could call his 'political' vision. Again a passage from Scholes's ***Structuralism in Literature*** sheds light on this construct and its nature: "A structuralist politic implies in particular a move away from adversary relationships in political processes at every level, to the extent that this is possible: away from combat between countries, between parties between factions, and above all between man and nature." And yet both *Nova* and *Triton*, in the conventional patterns that underlie their fictions, are built upon the necessity of just such combat or conflict: epic struggle and psychodrama. Scholes's messianic view would exclude what Western tradition calls tragedy. Delany explicity does not: "If SF is affirmative, it is not through any obligatory happy ending, but rather through the breadth of vision it affords through the complex interweave of these multiple visions of man's origins and his destinations. Certainly such breadth of vision does not *abolish* tragedy. But it does make a little rarer the particular needless tragedy that comes from a certain type of narrow-mindedness." On one hand, Delany's concept of tragedy is expansive: man must avoid the old patterns rather than blindly repeating them; thus he learns they are not binding in any absolute way. On the other, however, his view is contractive, for his heroes still follow the old hard way, the way of tragedy. Man must repeat the patterns that both myth and literary convention have set forth for him. Again, this is not inconsistency but intersection. From it comes that curious tension that gives Delany's best work its fascination and strength. For what he creates, at this point of tautness, is a new world in which the hero is both free and bound. Out of its construction (and his awareness or lack of awareness of his state) new truths about man can perhaps be glimpsed.

THE FALL OF THE TOWERS

The Fall of the Towers is a trilogy of novels begun in 1961 (when the author was nineteen) and completed in 1964. The three novels, in order of production and sequence, are: *Out of the Dead City* (originally called *Captives of the Flame*), *The Towers of Toron*, and *City of a Thousand Suns.* Despite certain excesses, *Towers* is a very accomplished piece of writing—indeed, it is hard to think of it as the product of a teenager. The first question that arises is: what kind of fiction is this? The answer to this query will show us the way to understanding Delany's later structures. In terms of the science fiction conventions it exploits, *Towers* is a highly unusual work. It is billed as space opera. Yet the reader of the cover copy is in for surprises when he opens the book. It is not a trilogy in the sense this "genre" calls for—the string of episodes, each written as a self-contained entity, and grouped in progressive fashion to mark off the steps in a hero's or society's development. On the contrary, *Towers* is clearly one novel—a long, densely-interwoven structure obviously conceived as a whole. Nor is it an "opera"—the usual panorama or "fresco" of colorful characters and events. In fact, all such spatializing terms, with their implication of surface superficiality, are inadequate here. There is, in *Towers*, a horizontal sweep, but this cross-movement is merely dynamic, not progressive. There is depth as well, not that of character or social analysis, but that of system—interlocking patterns, on many levels, engaged in ceaseless change.

Traditionally, the tripartite form stands for sequence transcended in balance and completion. Although man's actions invariably advance in a linear sense, and end in tragedy or death, they can at the same time be crowned by the order which is perfection. This rhythm of threes is seen as informing human development; by extension, it has come to regulate the evolution of man's societies and aspirations as well. Delany on the other hand, gives us a trilogy that, although it retains this basic pattern, suspends the anthropomorphic vision that traditionally lies behind it. In these three novels, neither heroes nor society evolve in any clear linear pattern. And yet, triads penetrate the texture of the work on all levels. This pattern is exploited for the dynamic ambiguity it contains; such groupings may be as easily stable as unstable. Three is an odd number; as such, it has an affinity with one. But here we meet the same ambiguity: is this the perfection of self-containment, or the instability of loneliness: Ones and threes decompose and recompose to form each other, plus compounds of two that are equally volatile—simultaneously harmony and contention. In the universe of *Towers*, there is neither progression nor stasis. Its various forms, human and social, undergo constant metamorphoses according to the set of basic patterns that abide. Men are free to choose order, but their choice does not necessarily control these patterns or shape them to their own wishes. In his use of the trilogy form, Delany gives us an ironic reflection of this deeper dynamic. The three titles promise a progression: Dead City, Human City, Radiant City. And in a sense, in the fall of the towers, this order is realized: the first two cities—rivals—sink so that the third can be born. Yet, in numerous counter-currents, as these three elements come together in different patterns, such order is lost. As various arrangements are played against each other, we see nothing less than the labyrinth of possibility.

In *Fall of the Towers*, human existence is presented in all its "multiplexity," where its numerous parts, on all levels, function in a bewildering variety of variational patterns. Delany's later works (with the exception of *Dhalgren*) will not improve on the maze. In this youthful novel, the system that is man and society develops with seemingly inexhaustible energy. If *Fall of the Towers* has a fault, it is a too abstract focus on the workings of this system to the exclusion of the flesh and blood people who "function" in it. Characters here are counters, little more than pieces in some great chess game. Delany's later works, while they continue to explore the dynamics of this human structure, also build upon the individual lives that must give flesh to the system. Gradually, counters become agents, and agents become human beings who feel and suffer. What Delany discovers is that this feeling and suffering becomes a powerful variable in the system. His best fiction creatively exploits a new tension: with one eye, man may see his world as an indifferent construct, a set of patterns; with the other, however, because he remains individual and mortal, man is forced to grasp it in existential terms.

Delany himself tells us *Towers* was conceived and executed as a whole. In an Afterword written in 1964, shortly after he completed the final section, the author explains the genesis of his work. The inspiration came to him one day in a flash: "That evening I wrote the first chapter of *Out of the Dead City* and planned the last chapter of *City of a Thousand Suns*. Over the next two years I orchestrated, harmonized, conducted. . . finally the ideas, incidents, and characters of that first chapter had staggered all the way through to the last." The structure of this group of novels is "musical." But what kind of musical structure does it resemble? Is it a theme and variations, or a sonata form? Do we have linear unfolding from an embryonic first chapter, or a circular return to the intial recapitulated statement? Both forms are present, and carefully superimposed. In time and space, this trio of novels is framed by a polar balance of opening and closing chapters. In themselves, each of these chapters is circular. The first begins as Jon ponders leaving Telphar, and ends as King Uske talks of sending spies back over the "transit ribbon" to the same "Dead City." The King speaks half-jokingly, for he believes the radiation in this city is still fatal. At the beginning, however, we see Jon miraculously alive in Telphar. Out of death comes life, for the radiation level falls, gradually allowing the dead city to renew itself. But it does so only to bring the death of this war the King is planning—the reborn city will be its focus and locus. The war does not run its course until the last chapter of the book. Even here a similar involuted circle is inscribed. Once again there is a leaving and returning to Telphar, but this time it is the same man, Vol the poet, who makes the journey. And his path is more broadly circular, for he returns via the City of a Thousand Suns. He touches neither town, however, but rejoins the radiation field that was pushed back at the beginning of the trilogy. As he does so, the reborn dead city, which alive has become the city of death, explodes, and dies once more. Vol's life comes full circle, so that the war which was itself a circle can be opened out.

Towers, as can be seen from the eccentric nature of these returns, moves forward at the same time it moves in a circle. In the complete edition of his trilogy, Delany reinforces these germinal opening and closing chapters with a prologue and epilogue. Here again things seem circular: the work begins and ends with the same man—Jon—leaving the same city—Telphar—for another. But is it the same city? Telphar has changed in the course of the novel. And doesn't Jon change as well? At least in the end he no longer goes alone—Alter is with him. And he goes this time to a different city—Toron has been replaced by the City of a Thousand Suns. New questions also arise: will not this latter city become in time another Toron, follow the same cycle in which the Arcadian reconstruction of a shattered world leads to dystopian perversion? And what of Jon? He has sought freedom throughout the book. Are not his new commitments simply new entrapments? Such labyrinthine ambiguity is the result of Delany's process: different individuals and situations are constantly fit into the same patterns, causing these to break down and reform in a vast variety of ways. Again, Delany's seminal chapters give an example. In both opening and closing, we find the same configurations—basic groups of one, two, or three. In each, however, as the elements change, the order and nature of these patterns are significantly different. The first chapter is overshadowed by Jon. As this lone survivor of the escape looks homeward, the reader journeys to Toron. On the way, we pass the City of a Thousand Suns—the triad of cities is complete. This grouping intersects with the triad of human types as Lug the Neanderthal and Quorl the telepathic giant discuss the men who build the radiant city. These triads in turn link with a series of polar combinations: the humans who build are set against those who have escaped from the mines, Quorl against Lug—antinomies that in time will be levelled or overturned. And there are other dualities based less on difference than on opposition or attraction: old Koshar talks with a rival merchant; Clea talks with her love Tomar. Each of these in turn will shift, and yet the binary pattern will abide. Born of this economic rivalry is a war that will lead to a new society of cooperation. And the fruit of this couple's love will be "randomax." The idea behind the game—as Clea develops it— leads to a war whose essence is not contact and conflict, but solipsism and random indifference.

In the last chapter Vol replaces Jon. The direction is merely reversed—the journey this time is from Toron to Telphar—but the pattern remains the same. Vol, like Jon, does not take the transit ribbon: but he does walk beside it. Jon doesn't reach Toron by the end of the first chapter; Vol never reaches his city—he passes the radiation barrier. Jon emerges from the radiation—life out of death; Vol re-enters it, coming full circle. The will to live and the will to die join. As Vol journeys, the same groupings of elements as before are encountered from a different angle. He passes again between the penal mines and the radiant city: this time, however, it is the latter that dominates. The same three cities are present, but now things are reversed: Toron is dead and Telphar waits to die. The landscape is seen as in a mirror, backwards. Where Jon was guided by the "Triple Being," Vol is followed by Arkor, one of that Being's former triple agents. Jon is an escaped criminal; but he is also the son of Toron's leading merchant, and as such is drawn to the sick city—hate is tempered by love. Vol too is a criminal, but he faces a different city, one beset with a contrary sickness. The social fabric of Toron is split and crumbling. Telphar possesses a deadly unity—indeed, the huge demented computer which inhabits it is the projection of Toron's psychotic desire for unity. And, as Telphar attacks Toron, turns on its creator, so Vol turns from Telphar. Vol is not attracted to the city; this lonely entity is attracted to him. But because it in turn mirrors his own deranged isolation, he is repelled by it. For the poet, this city too becomes a thing of love and hate—both "enemy" and lover who would cure itself in union with another. Vol, who has lost his beloved wife, yearns for such union. Yet he turns away and dies a lonely suicide, like the city and all those in the "war" whose sole enemy was their own psychotic fantasies. If Jon moves in like manner, he goes in a different direction. He seeks freedom, escaping from the mines. Then he turns around and goes on to new entanglements in the very city that put him there—a city that spurns yet needs him. As these patterns become clear, we see change itself caught up in a web of subtle balances.

Such abstract interplay of parts over a vast surface is more an art of arabesque than of narration. It forces us to read *Towers* less as a story, than a system of relationships. Indeed, what Delany calls "orchestration" occurs primarily on this level. At any given point we find him ordering his patterns on two planes simultaneously—vertical and horizontal. At first glance, Delany's trilogy could seem a typical space opera. Men's struggles in the island kingdom of Tormoron appear to be inexorably bound up in some cosmic battle that rages between the Triple Being and his adversary, The Lord of the Flames. Cover-copy writers may leap on this aspect to sell books. But to see Delany's book as space opera is to misconstrue it completely, and any reader who comes to it with this in mind must be extremely perplexed. What Delany actually is doing is using an old convention in a highly sophisticated manner. These overlords (of course) never tamper with the basic structure of a civilization: "We are a triple-lobed intelligence, and can touch up to three minds on any single world at once. The new creature can only have one agent on a world. . . So the battle will be won or lost within the framework of your own civilization." Clearly, that framework contains all the possibilities for this encounter of threes and ones. Tormoron is alone on Earth—the last enclave of humanity in the wake of some nuclear holocaust. Yet within this island world—which feeds itself exclusively on fish, and mines only one ore—have arisen three races, three cities. Man does not so much mirror these higher entities as they mirror him. In his world these extremes of isolation and perfection are given life, movement, the possibility of change by a dual rhythm—opposition or union—that is most human. One of Vol's prose poems puts this relationship—itself a tripartite order whose perfection contains the germ of its own dissolution—in the following terms: "These turreted cities at noon are the mind's ruined images—perfection, death, transition." Indeed, at various points of transition the world of *Towers* is constantly decomposing and reforming. In this process, singularity and trinity both become unstable states—intolerable and unattainable. Thus, among the three cities conflicts arise: two will die so that one may rise, its existence in turn menaced by new oppositions. Or one staple food becomes two contending ways of producing it. Roughly, there are two axes in *Towers*. Vertically, the intersection is situated at the point where reality meets dream—an epistemological intersection. Horizontally, the junction comes at the point where being and becoming, progression and stasis, overlap. We can call this the existential intersection.

The landscape of *Towers* has a surreal feeling, as if its texture were formed of the constant interpenetration of waking and dreaming states—the familiar world forever intersecting with something that transcends or suspends it. This occurs not only in the relations between the fantastic Triple Being and men in society—the ever-shifting interplay of italics and normal print on the page—but on the plane of purely human actions and situations as well. It is here we meet with strange mirrorings and recurrences, odd cases of *deja-vu*. There is a sense of characters endlessly reenacting the same patterns, in similar figurations echoing each other's movements. Further, the complexities of the dream-reality nexus on this level generate questions on another: the "war" fought throughout the second book of the trilogy, for instance, turns out to be a huge collective dream. The soldiers lie drugged in metal cells in the bowels of Telphar, the computer-city: "They are dreaming your war, each one desperately trying to dream his way back to what he knows is reality, somewhere deep in his mind." What we enter here is the labyrinth of human cognition. This war may be the image of men's mad fantasies; but whose mind does the computer reflect? Did the Lord of the Flames conceive it? Or is he (like his triple opponent) simply the image of our mind—"our psychotic fantasy?" The problem becomes one of knowing the real: "Why don't you just rack him [the Lord] up to one of those elements of reality that must be questioned to prove the reality real." We are forced in like manner to question each element of this work. What of the cities, the actors themselves? To Vol arises the possibility that these too exist only in the mind of a mad God: "We are the psychotic quips of a deranged cosmic mind, perhaps?" We pass off one transcendent relationship only to open out onto another. To this quandary, however, there are answers: just as the dream war results in real deaths, so this psychotic God allows moments of genuine union and perfection among the chaos of illusion. Once again, at this intersection of dream and reality, we are asked to read on the level of system. We cannot determine whether life is a dream, or whether the dream is a mad or a sane one, until we understand how these two elements interact—the system that governs their relationships one to the other. The focus of Delany's "surreal" narrative is less on states (waking or dreaming) than on transitions—the workings of the epistemological processes by which men relate to their universe.

We ask, as we read the shifting surface of *Towers*: is this a tale of one hero, two adversaries, or three races? There are many "battles" with the Lord of the Flames, and yet the essence of this singularity never materializes. The trio of "agents" pursue him through a series of metamorphoses, but each time they triangulate him and point "there," the scene fades. The Lord is more than a figment. It is as if each time he is held, isolation must explode to shatter order. The trio is constantly broken in these dream-attacks: if one is "killed," it is invariably Jon. But he is reborn at once in the "real" world. Indeed, this pattern of death and resurrection of the single hero is seen in the very beginning of *Towers*: Jon should have died in the radiation of Telphar. His escape from prison is crowned by a miracle in the first book as he leaves the dead city. In Book Three, he literally retraces his steps. Not only is Jon (in this symmetrically corresponding book) mirrored in inverse fashion by Vol (who courts death as he did life), but in a sense he mirrors his own actions as well. In his escape from the shark tank—in this fantastic setting we have a realistically drawn feat of heroism—he buys back his earlier supernatural escape with an act of free will. He saves Alter. And in another sense, his act is also reflected in the inverted mirror of Alter's previous deed—in the crumbling towers of Toron she had saved him as he does her. And like Jon, she does so also by reliving an encounter of Book One, and by redressing a "weakness." Her arm had been brutally shattered by the mad Queen Mother, and she had succumbed to pain and fear. Now, in the bedlam streets of Toron, she confronts and overcomes this same creature (and at the same time her own terror) by an act of will. In turn, these two free acts are seen, inversely, in the mirror of Jon's later cry of despair: "In this random chaotic world, filled with apes and demigods and all in between. . . where any structure you cling to may topple in a moment. . . and I am free—*what* am I free to do?"

The end result of this gallery of mirror distortions can be a vision of order as well as chaos. Such is the case with the evershifting patterns of the human races—apes, demi-gods and all between. In the beginning and end of *Towers*, the three races stand together. The pattern is static, taxinomic. With the final vision of the radiant city, the hierarchy is merely reversed: the Neanderthals enter first. But even in this procession—as fragments of the broken groups of each race reform and file in two by two—man remains the center of the structure, both mean and mystery. Elsewhere, the patterns of three are highly erratic, the triple order seemingly excluding all harmony between these races: Jon and the Duchess Petra combine with the giant Arkor; in the forest, Prince Let and the guard Quorl unite, not with an ape, but with the faceless mutant Tloto, who turns out himself (unlike even Quorl) to be telepathic. This surprising reversal should prepare us for others on a larger scale. The only other place in *Towers* where all three races interact, and function as one humanity, is (surprisingly) in the vast central section—the no man's land of the dream-war. This union is shattered as the dream explodes—shortly before, in the course of its random progress, Quorl and Tel, giant and human had both died. Only Lug the ape survives. Out of this paradox [is harmony among human types possible only at the heart of chaotic dream?] will come further reversals that lead to higher order. In the barracks of this dream/battlefield, men fleece Lug at "randomax," only to be bested in turn by the superior minds of the telepaths. A war that was intended to isolate becomes, in spite of itself, a meeting of minds. And such correctives as this one, apparently, are beneficial in an evolutionary sense, for later in the City of a Thousand Suns the tables are turned. A young Neanderthal undercuts another human soldier's desire to "take" him by elucidating the laws behind "randomax" with mathematical precision.

One of the things that gives *Towers* its floating, dream-like landscape is the continual reappearance of characters in different configurations. We see the giant Quorl in the beginning—he is one of the prison "guards" Jon eludes. He reappears later, first with Prince Let, then with Tel. Jon had fled not only from Quorl but from a woman guard named Larta. Later he joins with Arkor to combat the Lord of the Flames; in the end, Arkor unites with this same Larta to enter the City of Suns. This sense of *deja-vu*, on the level of characters, is occasionally made even stronger. An example is the mirror twins, Prince Let and

Tel the fisher boy. Their opposition on the social scale is caught up and fixed in the inversion of letters in their respective names. Not only are these two linked by Quorl, but both die, if in different places and circumstances, at exactly the same juncture between dream and reality. Like their names, the situations of their deaths are exactly reversed. As Tel dies on the battlefield, he has assumed the role of the aristocratic scout Quorl, and at the same time forged a new bond of sympathy with Lug. Earlier in the forest (also with Quorl), Let too had felt an attraction to the creature Tloto. Tloto saves Let's life, prefiguring the rise of the Neanderthal to nobility of mind in the middle book. Tel's death in "battle," however, is both different and similar to Let's in the falling towers of Toron. Tel aspires to lead; Let, on the contrary, throws off his rank, embracing the common condition of Tel: "Remember that boy, Petra, who told me about the sun coming up over the sea? . . . Well, for him, then, we'll sail straight into the morning. Whoever he was, we'll sail for him." His change comes at the same time as Petra, the renegade aristocrat, is reconciled with the aristocracy. In this echoing series of reversals, it is as if each person reaches for another and misses. In another way, similarities and differences intersect. Just as Tel is set against the "brute" Lug, who will later rise to solve the "randomax" problem, so Let is linked in his last moment with a different sort of beast—a debased human, the paranoiac Jeof. Set against the idyllic futility of Let's voyage into morning, Joef's mad dream ("Have they come for me?") detonates the bomb that destroys them all. Here, as with Tel, there is explosion at the point where dream and reality meet. In these two mirror-names, differences and sameness intertwine and then recede as in a gallery of reflections. In like manner, Clea Koshar spells her name backward—Rashok—and becomes a different person. Yet it is because of this difference that she is able to find herself again.

But if the intersection of dream and reality can lead to death, it leads to perfection as well. Another question arises: is *Towers* a tale of three cities or of two? Against the three cities of Tormoron are set the mirror cities Jon encounters as he journeys back and forth between the realm of the Triple Being and Earth. After escaping from the penal mines, he reaches Telphar. But this is not the earthly city—above it two suns shine. And here the towers only "symbolize" death—Jon lives to return to Toron. Later in Book One, he again finds himself at the gates of this other Telphar: this time he sees a city that is both dead and alive, endlessly building itself. The dream aspect of the place is openly stated: "The city responds to the psychic pressures of those near, building itself according to the plans. . . and techniques of whatever minds press it into activity." Jon wants to rebuild his life. For him, contact with this dream city brings forth new life, as one plane of existence spills over into the other. In a later dream episode, however, this same contact brings death. After pursuing the Lord of the Flames through a series of metamorphoses, the three agents enter this Telphar of two suns in their own forms. As they apply "psychic pressure" to isolate the Lord, the city explodes. On the other side of the universe, at the same time, the dead Earth city comes alive. The polarity is more complex yet. Under the two suns, destruction is linked with perfection, the union of three. On Earth the reborn Telphar is joined with war and chaos.

Book One is dominated by this transit between the two Telphars, dream and reality. But which is which? The connection made in Book Two, between Toron and Telphar on Earth, only reinforces this ambiguity. Here the transit ribbon plies not only between two cities but between a psychotic society and its dream-war. The cities of the first part are worlds apart and yet connected. Here they are physically joined, yet separated. Isolation ends only when the mind-net links all humanity in the terrible question: what war? The same triple agents appear to force this revelation. They trap the old enemy in a new, human form. Again there is an "explosion"—simultaneous imposition and disintegration of order. In the shock of recognition—were we capable of dreaming this random horror?—each man suddenly finds himself more alone than ever before. This heightened consciousness of the human condition leads to deeper loneliness. From this (again simultaneously) come both constructive acts and destructive—new unions and works of the mind, and the rage of the mad computer that will topple more towers: the twinned cities this time.

In the first book of the trilogy, the isolation (whose symbol is the Lord of the Flames) is given substance in Jon Koshar: his confused search both to be free and yet belong is mirrored in the invisible wanderings through Toron and his father's house—he does not communicate, but remains physically close. In the second book, this isolation is embodied in the computer-city and its "war." In the third, it is again incarnate in an individual—Vol Nonik and his lonely yearning. Jon ultimately gives himself form and flesh through his actions, and breaks out of the dream. In pursuing the "enemy," this invisible man unites with others—in the end he can again face his father as a son. The computer shatters its dream through hate: in place of imaginary battles, it begins to throw real bombs. In this way too, connections are made, for its hate is the obverse of love. The machine proves this when it destroys itself out of sympathy for Vol. Only this one human is doomed to remain alone, to establish links in spite of himself. Vol approaches the problem of dream and reality on two fronts: art and violence, construction and destruction. On both, however, his stance remains negative—avoidance rather than commitment. In his eyes, poetry must probe the reality of suffering: "The great poet explores the inflamed lips of ruined flesh with ice-caked fingers. . . but ultimately his poem is the echoing, dual voice reporting the damage." But the poem here remains an echo, shadow and not substance. Indeed, Vol himself cannot maintain such impassibility—he erupts into violence. Leaping on the transit ribbon, he would flee the reality of this pain. All he succeeds in doing is moving in a circle. But his actions force the union of Telphar and Toron, metal brain and human creator: there is a double explosion—the two cities crumble so that the new city of suns may rise. Only Vol's death releases him from the dream, and it is a reality beyond recall. This final death sends us back across the trilogy to its dream-beginning: a man who should have died stands in the other Telphar. There is no transit ribbon, and yet somehow he reaches Toron. Here, in fact, at this initial nexus of two worlds—supernatural and familiar—a new transit ribbon begins. A band of semi-precious stones—the *leitmotif* that recurs throughout the books in connection with the "higher" beings—threads its way through the three novels, only to make its final twist (like Delany's later helix) on the vision of the radiant city. A passage has been made: we have order, but not freedom from change. The dream-city was both building and dying. So it will be with its new twin: "Free to build or destroy they, too, approached the City of a Thousand Suns, to be struck by blue smoke. . . the red of polished carbuncle. . . the green of beetles' wings."

On its horizontal axis, *Towers* seems a construct that both moves and fails to move—simultaneous progression and stasis. The plot "develops"—a war is fought and terminated, the Triple Being comes to understand its adversary, Jon and Vol search and find life and death respectively. And yet, that development only reaffirms patterns present from the start—in this sense, the action illustrates the endlessly shifting polarity of threes and ones, perfection and death, that lies at the heart of the book. Only in the broadest sense, however, does this describe the linear dynamics of the work, the relation of its three sections one to another. The actual interplay is far more subtle. The first novel is marked by movement: if there is anything permanent here, it is the necessity of triadic groups to decompose and reform. The second, in contrast, is marked by stasis: the focus here is the "war," the action being centered on two battlefields of the mind—Toron and the no-man's-land. These two sections appear to balance: in one, threes dissolve into ones; in the other, threes are caught up in one, held in suspension like the three races in battle. Throughout the two books this equilibrium is countered and undermined by a steady progression of events: there are losses that cannot be balanced within this dual framework, and must spill over into the third novel. The relation of the terminal book to the first two is more complex still. In one sense, these three parts seem to inscribe a closed form ABA, in which the patterns of the last book mirror those of the first. In another, however, the form seems open and progressive, an ABC where the third part provides climactic resolution for the configurations woven in the first and subsequently developed throughout. *Towers* can indeed be read either way. At the point where these two senses of form overlap—the third book—the process of reading must shift to a new, analytical level. What may previously have seemed merely abstract patterns—change and permanence, statis and progression—now become a different problem: that of the relationship between individual human existences and a changeless (but ever-changing) system. Out of the interplay between death and perfection on this horizontal, existential plane comes a new set of terms to be opposed or balanced: chaos and order. When the broken patterns of the final book seem to reform in random fashion, and newly-formed patterns randomly break down, we are drawn to ask why. Delany prompts more than answers. For even if we see the underlying order, can it redeem the chaos of an individual life? And can we ever see or understand that order entirely? Delany's analytical structure forces us to examine the part chaos plays in the system of existence.

Book One exists under the sign of change—patterns of threes endlessly break and reform. These are often family units: the Queen Mother and her two sons; the fisher couple and their son Tel; Jon, Clea, and Old Koshar. Two of these are already broken as the novel begins: the fisherman searches for his runaway son; Jon is in the penal mines. The third will soon be broken—Prince Let is abducted. But of these floating elements new trios form. Tel unites with Rara and her niece Alter in the Devil's Pot, the slums of Toron. This group in turn will be split; its disbanding is linked with the breaking up of another. Alter is responsible for the abduction of Let; she is caught and her arm smashed by the Queen Mother. With Tel and the old man Geryn, Alter had formed another trio, of conspirators. The latter is broken when Geryn dies, only to be reformed again around a new third term: Arkor the giant spirits the two children away, and joins with them in telepathic union. Against this ever-changing dance of threes in Book One, the central trio of "agents" is gradually forming. Jon's career begins with a three-man escape from the mines. Two are killed, but Jon is spared to become the first emissary of the Triple Being. At the ball in old Koshar's house, he moves between his sister and the Duchess Petra, who calls him by name. These two join with a third to pursue the Lord of the Flames through a variety of triple forms. The trine is complete, however, only at that moment when these three finally know each other, at the moment when each comes to know himself. Union coincides with dissolution as each individual stands together and yet alone. The triple masks fall away, and with them the freedom of metamorphosis: "I guess it was what I was wearing when I became me, too. That was the time when freedom seemed most bright."

If the basic pattern of Book One is three, that of Book Two is one. Three races are caught up in one war, one computer network. They are freed from this only by being taken up in the larger telepathic web that extends over all of Tormoron. One-in-three becomes three-in-one. At the very center of this multiplicity in unity sits Tel's pet, the shapeless ball of feathers that weaves its way constantly between the battlefield destinies of Lug, Quorl and Tel. Yet, just as the threes prove unstable, so do these ones: the mind-net makes each man more alone in his guilt and fear than he was before. At the basis of both these figures is a similar binary tension. As individuals, Jon, Petra, and Arkor are all split beings: a humanitarian duchess, a pariah telepath. This instability causes each of them to reach out for union with some other being. The trine breaks down into a series of pairs: Jon-Alter, Petra-Let, Arkor reaching out in loneliness for Vol. In a sense, Tel's pet also mirrors this dynamic inner division. It is one creature, yet, as its ever-shifting name implies (flip-flop, flep-flup), is constantly changing and dividing. Linking both books is this same instability of oneness, loneliness ever striving to new union. Against it runs a counter-current, loss. Clea, in Book One, loses Tomar; in Book Two, Alter loses Tel; in Book Three, Vol loses Renna. This binary rhythm of loss and reunion is, once again, both fixed and unfolding. Tel's pet, at the center of the central book, is its emblem and point of stasis. The overlapping careers of Jon and Vol, stretching all across the trilogy, are its dynamic axis, the linear thrust that carries *Towers* from one end to the other.

In Book Three, losses that seemed irreplaceable are nevertheless replaced: Clea joins with Rolth Catham, Alter with Jon. These unions may appear random, but in reality are not. Jon is able to escape from the fish tank—and thus save Alter and recreate his own earlier evasion in terms of controlled human action—only because he has learned acrobatics from the white-haired girl. And when Clea and Catham come together, theory and history unite—from this mutual exchange each goes on to finish his *oeuvre*. Indeed, at first glance in this third book, order appears to emerge from chaos on all levels. A new trio of "agents" arises to replace the one that has dissolved. The Triple Being finally strikes a balance with his cosmic adversary. Even the unions of the final vision of the radiant city—Rara with Old Koshar, for instance—

are more than a random patching-together of left-over pieces: in these two persons, the extremes of the old suspended social order unite. Amidst all this harmony there remains one false note—Vol. Vol touches many of these new patterns with a solvent or corrosive action. In the new trio formed by Clea, Catham and himself, he is the weak point. Catham overcomes the handicap of his half-destroyed head, learning to live in his transparent skull. Vol cherishes his broken hand, and remains a cripple, an odd number, a broken pair. Like these others, he too has lost his beloved companion, in brutal and absurd fashion. But why can he not find another? His poetry perhaps holds the answer. His famous line, which runs through this last book like a musical motif, is twisted into a form that mirrors its creator. It reads like a maze in which each spark of hope is subsequently muffled by despair: "Caged by the over-muscled heart, we are trapped in that bright moment where we learned our doom, but still we struggle, knowing, too, that freedom is imposed the very moment when the trap springs. . . shut." The words express an iron determinism. And the segment of this line used as a slogan—and painted on the walls of Toron—inscribes a dreadful circle, in which the "bright moment" is hopelessly held between "trapped" and "doom." And yet, as these verbal convolutions extend in linear fashion throughout the narrative, they invariably intersect with life. An example is the fact that this slogan is written on different walls in different ways. As Jeof stops Kino's hand, a chance event fixes part of this phrase in a thoroughly random manner. Words that, prescriptively, would deny all human freedom are in fact open to articulation, and not only by blind chance but through human choice as well. Men learn, in fact, that they have the freedom to snip this line where they will. As Vol's mind weaves this extended statement, events stop him on the word "springs." At this point the trap—verbal and otherwise—can either open or shut. He has the choice to stop or continue. To push on to perfection, in this case as in others, is certain death.

Clea's "bright moment" hovers on the same edge. Her flash of insight—that the war is non-existent—is inexorably bound with the deep-seated pain of Tomar's loss, and even deeper fears that her theoretical discoveries led to this random nightmare. The bonds that form are unthinkable: her ideas are fertilized by Tomar, who introduces her to "randomax." Is the mysterious game itself the projection of a sick collective psyche? Beyond pain and even guilt, she faces the abyss of man's yearning for chaos and destruction. In her case, however, to know doom is not to be trapped in it. She opts for order instead—Catham and the unified field theory. Arkor's moment is similar—his miraculous expansion of telepathic powers yields an inconsolable vision of human isolation, loneliness magnified a thousandfold. Again, he looks on chaos only to choose life, union , and order: empathy rather than negation. Later, he reaches out through telepathically-felt pain for Vol—his loneliness at the barrier is tempered by tears of compassion. In the final vision, he takes Larta, is reconciled with his fellow telepaths, and enters the City. In each case, at the central moment both order and chaos are potentially there; man can choose either. Vol's choices, on the other hand, are clearly negative. He rejects his poems: "To feed on destruction, bloating to greatness. . . they're not worth it!" He refuses contact—with the computer, with Arkor. In his elliptical last journey, Vol does not face his moment so much as run away from it. The moment comes anyway: his escape into words, into the labyrinth of his famous line, suddenly issues into real doom. He continues his word-screen: "The barrier. . ., " only to discover that he has already crossed it, the radiation barrier from which there is no return. Refusal to choose turns out to be a choice after all. In relation to his line, Vol has shaped only his own destiny, no other. Each makes his own world.

In this final hour, Vol's refusal is balanced by Jon's triple choice. Through it he will, in a sense, redeem the broken triads of both Book One and Book Three. Jon's "bright moment" seems to be an act of negation equal to Vol's: he is free, but to do what? Through his deeds, however, he has already answered this question. He has saved Alter, and she him—they have given each other the gift of life. Now he answers again—this time with an act of intellect. He does so by facing another dilemma: perfection in human art and science. How can these express the ideal if they are created by beings who themselves are imperfect and mortal? The three works of Clea, Catham and Vol—the unified field theory, the revised history, the poems—are all born of pain, division, death. And yet they were all written, Catham tells Jon, not to "try to teach people how to be ideal," but rather "to acknowledge that man, with all this chaos. . . can be ideal." Jon finds a new answer to his question: he is "free to try and achieve that ideal, or not to try." The way he chooses is to try and become the "ideal reader," and by so doing to forge a union that otherwise cannot exist. This trio of artists and thinkers is unstable—it collapses. But even if they themselves do not abide, the trinity of their works may yet survive, at least in the mind of Jon.

If the opposition of Jon and Vol creates patterns that link the beginning and end of this trilogy, another key opposition connects the middle with its extremities. *Towers* begins with Jon moving away from the "barrier," in search of order and meaning; it ends with Vol's chaotic plunge across it into no-man's-land and meaningless death. At the heart of the book, in this same no-man's-land "beyond the barrier," is born something that will gradually evolve in the opposite direction, and ultimately cause Vol's night to be illuminated by the City of a Thousand Suns. Here at the core of the dream-war—where both illusion and chaos are sanctioned by human reason—the lowly Neanderthal pierces the web of lies, and starts humanity back on the road to civilization and order. Quorl the giant has put up a sign in the wilderness: "This way home." But where is home for these three representatives of a divided race? They are together, and yet remain in physical and mental isolation one from the other. To Quorl the sign represents a yearning. Not only has the war uprooted him from his native forest, but it has divided his people as well, separating telepaths from non-telepaths. Tel is a homeless runaway, the victim of an economic system that has made orphans of half the men of Tormoron. But because he has found a substitute family—Rara and Alter—he can ask the question "what is home?" This is the spark that triggers Lug. Because of his primitive roots, he is able to make a distinction that is essential here—between home and not-home. Working out from these rudiments of a logical system, he controls the random factors of this landscape, and reduces them to order. This leads to a breakthrough: "No sun. . . No moon. Home is where I live, and then there is the rest of the wide world. but where is this? . . Noplace." The process here moves from one to two to three. Vol's trinity is rearranged: death, transition, perfection. This merest seed of logic blossoms later in the story as the young Neanderthal (Lug's son?) reduces "randomax" to order. Here again, at the center, a triad decomposes to give rise to a new balance: Quorl makes a suicidal attempt to reach the "enemy"—his act (like Vol's) is a flight from reality into despair; Tel dies randomly, senselessly on the verge of life: he is about to "go home." In the stately procession that crowns the new order of the radiant city, the Neanderthals enter first—not by threes or twos or ones, but as a family. In this embryonic world, they will provide the same center of gravity as they did for the old Tormoron. This does not, of course, make it any more permanent or immune from change. In a world where humanity is still free to build or destroy, the Triple Being's final words promise no finality: "The wound has at least been cauterized, and you may go home now, and attempt to heal." The Neanderthals at least have shown where home might be.

Towers then is a marvellously constructed work—hardly a matter of "staggering through" to the end. If anything, it is over-constructed. What we have essentially is a logician's design, in which both the surreal and human axes converge to expose a problem which is neither epistemological nor existential, but essentially logical in nature. The ape who explains "randomax" says: "If you perceive all the factors accurately, it isn't random at all." Three times in three books such total perceptions are made: we discover all the factors in the game, in the war, and in the struggle between the Triple Being and the Lord of the Flames. The Lord is explained in the following terms: "As we equate aloneness and isolation with death, so it equates bringing individuals. . . together as death, for when this happens their actual physical beings explode." But does this "reverse polarity" really explain all we have witnessed here? We have seen death in the human world produced both out of aloneness and unison—the *Liebestod* of Vol and the computer is one example of the latter. And if oneness is still death for Vol, it is the beginning of life for Jon. We have each time a more and more inclusive system; each time we encounter the Goedelian Law—in terms of any given system, there is no freedom from inconsistency. If we think there is, we find ourselves trapped, as in Vol's "bright moment." Indeed, each of the bright moments that reveal a system are intersections that lead in unpredictable directions—the end of the false war leads to real bombing, the new ordered city opens out on the possibility of destruction as well as construction.

In *Towers* the reader sees more of the system than the characters who live it. For us the interplay of change and permanence, order and chaos, would seem to be explained by the triple rhythm: perfection, death, transition. the formula is Vol's but does he understand its centrality to the world he lives in? Who discovers, for instance, the true nature of the war—is it Lug from inside the system, or the Triple Being from outside? In analagous fashion, who discovers the nature of the Lord of the Flames? Is the exposure made by its human antagonists (and as a result of their sacrifices), or by the author himself? The answer comes to us in the last pages, *ex machina*: the relation of the voice from the whirlwind to the actors is ironic. From beyond the bounds of the novel, in the Afterword, the author comments on the meaning of his system: "For what it's worth, Vol never did see, and at the end, though he is in control—so to speak—of his death, Catham is in control of his life. So there." Is this voice meant to be any more authoritative? The real problem of *Towers*—and of this kind of ironic system-building in general—is again expressed by Vol: "Yes, when we know everything the random disappears, but while we're finding out we still have to deal with it somehow." We might believe he understands these words, were he more fully realized as an individual, a suffering man for whom we could feel pity and fear. Delany's characters are only potentially interesting here—in the end, they remain counters in a vast game, puppets in the hands of the Romantic ironist. Still, *Towers* is a marvelously realized beginning, a work which thoroughly explores the dynamics of a human system. In a series of later novels, Delany will loosen the web, expand upon the minds and feelings of his heroes and heroines as they too "deal with" the random. He moves toward the much more subtle balance of man and system which will mark a work like *Nova.*

FROM BABEL-17 TO NOVA

Three novels, *Babel-17* (1966), *The Einstein Intersection* (1967), and *Nova* (1968), form a whole in Delany's canon and represent what is probably his best work to date. All of these novels are relatively short. In complexity and intricacy of design, however, they equal *Towers*, and even surpass it in many respects. If the early trilogy remains abstract—an anatomy of the system that underlies human existence on both the individual and collective level—it nonetheless exposes the themes that Delany will explore in the sharper analytical focus of these later works. In *Towers*, within the coordinates of change and permanence, chaos and order, various relationships appear: language to reality, freedom to order, art to crime or violence. More firmly rooted in the destiny of an individual hero, these themes are given flesh and bones in *Babel* and its successors.

This deeper probing comes from a change of perspective, most radically visible in *Babel*. The structure contracts and polarizes around a single point—the individual and his quest. Already the world of *Towers* is strangely constricted. Its base is an isolated island world. In this small compass all the various functions of the system are potentially there; gradually, as more and more elements interconnect, the microcosm expands to fill a universe of relationships. The base upon which *Babel* rests is rather different. Here it is the individual man who reaches out to fill the space between himself and another. And the reaching out, this time, is horizontal. The form of this novel, ostensibly, is that of the linear quest.

The patterns of circle and web are of course implicit in the structure of *Towers*. In each of these new novels, however, they not only dominate, but are dominated by the hero's quest—they have become living, energized forms. In *Babel* and the other works, the hero progresses in linear fashion, and at the same time remains static. He may wander from world to world, and return to the same geographic place from which he started. Yet somehow he meets himself, tying together the loose ends of his existence. This moment can be either destructive or creative: he can lock himself in, or break out by reaching another. The same is true with the web. The focus in *Babel* is not on randomness or order so much as how the individual (in Vol's words) "deals with" these. It is true that Jon, in *Towers*, is a questing figure. But his function is that of a thread: he is woven, moved back and forth on a shuttle of fixed points. In the three newer novels, the questing hero has become the maker and breaker of webs. This new hero is artist as well as actor. In *Towers*, the seeker (Jon) and the poet (Vol) were separate destinies. Now they become one. Even in *Nova* this is true, for Lorq von Ray is not simply surrounded by artists, he is symbiotically united with them in the ordeal of the quest.

In *Towers*, the function of art is merely discussed, in terms of how it orders the randomness of existence, how the pain of that ordering, the experience of order in chaos, in turn destroys the artist. *Babel* and its two successors act out the process of artistic creation itself. Each follows a similar pattern. On the surface there is action and adventure. Within these conventional forms, however, the accent shifts in a most unconventional manner—away from the external world of deeds toward a much more private battlefield, where the hero struggles to give communicable order to words. In the beginning, in Delany's universe, is the word. If you can't name a thing, says Rydra Wong in *Babel*, how can you think about it? Not only does language affect the way each man perceives reality, but for each man reality is first and foremost a linguistic phenomenon. In these novels, the hero discovers his place in the world only when he establishes solid links between word and object. Almost at once, in *Babel*, the fight to stem the invader modulates; the voyage of the *Rimbaud* becomes the exploration of the problems of human communication in a fallen and divided world. What in *Einstein* seems but another variant of the Grail legend, or the Orphic quest for life renewal, turns out to be something else—the search to name objects in a world whose linguistic (and thus behavioral and mythical) parameters are unclear and unknown. The quest in *Nova* is similar. The economic warfare, and even the mythic act of fire-stealing, cover something else—the hero's search to fix the unnameable, the "heterotropic" Illyrium that is "many things to many people." This process is artistic as well as linguistic. In these novels, the quest for meaning in a world of verbal multiplicity is simultaneously a search to control the language structure as well. Not only are the webs which are made or broken essentially verbal ones, but the shadow each character casts is primarily a language shadow. Of these, the hero's is merely the biggest and most inclusive. In the same way, his story is the biggest circle. The artist-hero solves his problem, or reaches his goal and closes the circle of action only to open another: he is ready to write the work we have just finished reading. In this sense, these novels are more optimistic than *Towers*, for even if (as with Lorq von Ray) the individual succumbs, his work abides—we hold it in our hands.

As with *Towers* (but to quite different ends), *Babel-17* takes a number of stock SF themes and situations and shapes them into a new construct. Old familiar elements are given new functions, and we are prevented from suspending disbelief, and forced to read the tale on a level both ironic and analytical. We have all the paraphernalia of the space opera here: interplanetary war, spies, secret languages, space battles, and exotic beings and "cultures" of the sort Alfred Bester (an acknowledged influence) peoples his teeming universes with. The fact that Delany's superhero, Rydra Wong, is a woman does not deviate from tradition. Heinlein's world encompasses two types of female—scatterbrain and amazon, do-nothing and do-everything. Rydra's lineage derives from the latter: she is beautiful, a prodigy in the field of linguistics, and at twenty-six the most read poet in the "worlds of five galaxies." She knows (and uses) karate, and can captain a space ship (she even has her license). She saves her ship from destruction with a bag of marbles and her native genius. There are other commonplaces. Babel-17 as a language descends from Heinlein's "speedtalk"—in it the thinking process is faster and more efficient ("any other tongue seems clumsy beside it"). Baron Ver Dorco is a well-known type of mad scientist. In his genetic engineering he unites Dr. Frankenstein with another archetype, Pygmalion. He is the obsessed "artist" in search of the perfect human being, the creator of beauty monstrous in its lack of a human soul. In more ways than one, his "creation" is linked to him by fatal bonds of love and hate. Even Delany's final scene is traditional: the heroine and other articulate figures gather (like Holmes and Dr. Watson) to fit the final pieces into the puzzle, and explain the mystery of Babel-17 to their audience.

Delany makes sophisticated use of this material. Fabulous hero, super-language, the final shedding of light—all these elements belong traditionally to the celebration of reason, the triumph of will. In *Babel*, however, he uses the energies of space adventure to probe a contrary notion: the divided state that resulted from just such scientific presumption—the first Babel and the fall that drove men and their languages apart. Rydra's primary task is to unite men, not to conquer them. Her battle cry, "I'm going to solve this whole Babel-17 business myself," ironically leads inward, not outward. The language she sets out to investigate proves a most paradoxical thing—it is a formidable weapon and a marvelous instrument of communication at one and the same time. What separates men can (and will) be used to join them as well. Also, the pursuit of Babel's mystery leads inexorably to the mystery of self: this language that lacks a word for "I" forces the heroine to examine the nature of her own "I." And at the heart of self she discovers another paradox, that of the communication process itself: the "I" must be abandoned to another, a "you," before it can be known at all.

Playing on this disparity between conventional expectations and fictional reality, Delany manipulates the reader. In *Babel*, we run the gamut of genres—from epic beginning to tragic middle to comic end. The opening pages announce the public task, and enumerate the heroine's strengths; the middle contracts to a very private struggle—the superwoman recognizes her human weaknesses. The final scene tempers heroic bravado with muted comedy. The extent to which Rydra's powers have been qualified is mirrored in her joking promise to defend the Butcher: ''And even without Babel-17, you should know by now, I can talk my way out of anything.'' In this novel Delany would lead the reader to seek the common humanity that lies beneath both the superhuman and pseudo-human. The landscape of *Babel* abounds with''cosmeti-surgical''monsters, who have altered their human form for reasons that seem mainly aesthetic. There are ''discorporate'' shades floating about, and ''perverted'' unions of three, oftentimes mixes of living beings and resurrected dead. Not only does each of these strange figures find his place in the vast web of humanity that Rydra weaves, but all have the same basic human need—to communicate with another. The hardest to integrate, in fact, are paradoxically the most ''normal'' beings, the bureaucrats of Customs and Administration. This diverse landscape for the eye and ear is the mirror of Babel—the fallen and divided world. Indeed, there is imagery of the fall through-out the novel: from the Edenic worm of Rydra's poem, to her innate flaws (the consummate linguist who stutters, the strong-woman who swoons), to the missing letter in Customs Agent Danil D. Appleby's name. Even Appleby, smug as he is represents an imperfect being in need of others. And he falls quite literally—he is ''hustled'' by a succubus in the discorporate quarter. This (and Rydra's example) leads him in the end to undergo minor cosmeti-surgery, to alter his body. If this is a fall, it is (for Appleby as for all others in the novel) a fortunate one: it leads men to cross the boundaries of intolerance, to seek mutual understanding.

In accordance with its titular image, *Babel* conceives of the fall of man primarily in linguistic terms. But here too we have the *felix culpa*, for differences in language separates men, only to unite them all the more firmly in the end. Thus, Rydra purposely forces the disconsolate Navigators Ron and Calli (who have lost their ''third'') to take another who speaks no English. In struggling to overcome the language barrier, they learn to love another person again. The vision of language that underlies the novel encompasses isolation and error, but not predestination. Vol's hopeless determinism in *Towers* remains a language maze; men are free to snip this thread of words where they will. In *Babel*, there are both imperfect languages and the possibility of a perfect one. The book's epigraph states the problem thus: ''If our knowledge of speech, or the speech itself, is not yet perfect, neither is civilization." It is possible, then, to some extent at least, to redeem this fall through a man-made world of communication. "What you perceive you change," Rydra tells Butcher, "but *you* must perceive it." Rydra's quest will be a quest for knowledge: this is the goal of everyman's search. This is not arrogant overreaching science, but humble building, for the key to such perception is knowledge of self. Language in *Babel* is essentially "speech"; at the basis of each system is a speaker. Many of the characters in this novel create their own linguistic "world"—the texture of *Babel* is a multitude of such "tongues," manners or modes of speaking. Indeed, as Rydra and Butcher discover, men can control what they name, but only if they can name themselves first. It is by knowing themselves that they are able to "name" the Invasion, seeing this war for what it is—an empty mirror that simply magnifies basic human isolation and loneliness. Delany tells us in the Afterword to *Towers* that his trilogy got its name form a series of drawings "depicting different groups of people reacting to some catastrophic incident never shown." The war in that novel has no substance beyond a slogan: it vanishes as soon as it is named—"what war?" At the core of this false collectivity there are only isolated, encapsulated individuals, who break out to psychic destuction or (as in the case of Lug) communication. In *Babel* war again turns out to be essentially a linguistic entity; as such, it must be "fought" on the level of language. The "espionage ring," in fact, turns out to be a circle that closes on itself—a tautology. The same "spies" are redirected when the "enemy" is renamed. In like manner, Babel-17 can be both a weapon and the key to ending the war: seen in the light of this superior analytical language, it reveals its true nature—another redundancy. The word for "Alliance" in Babel is "one-who-has-invaded"—the two sides appear in a self-cancelling mirror. The new language simply shows us what was under our noses all along, but obfuscated in a screen of words: both sides are men, the Invader capital, Nueva-nueva York is but a dialectical variant of our own major city. All the apparatus of the space opera and interplanetary war vanish as the language circle closes on a common humanity. Identical messages are placed on the commanders' desks in the two capitals: "This war will end within six months." This possibility will in time be semantically imprinted in minds on both sides—what is named will come to be.

Rydra, however, is a poet as well as a linguist. Her "talent" is a special use of language, one necessary for her quest. In the many levels or layers of action in *Babel*, we have space adventure, an old-fashioned love story, and a tale of the artist's development. At the outset Rydra is already a famous poet; this prodigy still desires to grow as an artist. Indeed, her initial view of the poet's task is one-sided: "You know what

I do? I listen to other people, stumbling about with their half thoughts and half sentences and their clumsy feelings they can't express, and it hurts me. So I go home and burnish it and polish it. . . .I know what they want to say, and I say it for them." The inadequacies of these gropings as a process of communciation are seen in her first meeting with General Forester. She sees his love for her, but cannot help him in his frustrated isolation. And he cannot enter her: "Not a thing, you're still safe. . . Didn't communicate a thing at all." On the plane of artistic creation, monologue becomes dialogue only when she enters Butcher's mind, and gazes on new, terrifying areas of her own being in the mirror of another. At this moment, she learns the inadequacy of her old talent. In this mutual exchange her words are "ignited"; she grows as person and as artist. And it is this latter growth which leads in the end to reversal of the Forester situation. Because T'mwarba has learned her art of reading "body-language," he is able to enter her and break the autistic union with Butcher, striking a bridge between this closed universe of Babel-17 and the language world of ordinary humans. In exploring new regions, the poet has nevertheless sown the seeds that, once they germinate, enable others to bring her back again. Rydra not only controls the system of human communication (thus saving her world), but she also reveals its workings as well. That revelation is *this* novel—the novel Rydra is going to write.

The broadest view of Rydra's actions comes from the most shadowy member of her crew, the discorporate "Eye": "She cut through worlds, and joined them—that's the important part—so that both became bigger." If the central rhythm of *Towers* is ternary, here this binary dynamic of cutting and joining, breaking and making, dominates. In *Babel* the extremes of *Towers*—perfection and death—are given a different spatial relationship: that of circle and center. The circle can be both harmony and confinement. At its center lies a restless, devouring hunger that seeks to shatter it: there is a worm in Eden, a traitor in the circle of the ship's crew. But once again this fallen state can be fortunate. Hunger not only destroys men but leads them to break the circle of self, to reach out from the prison of language in new directions, opening the closed system. This process is illustrated as Rydra traces the great circles with her marbles at the core of the blind ship. Because great circles intersect ("all great circles have to have at least two points in common"), she is able to calculate the trajectory that will break the fatal orbit around Earth. In like manner, the intersection of two other "great circles," Rydra and Butcher, at the heart of the novel (where they quite literally join at the two common points of "I" and "you"), permits them to escape the enclosure of self and language, becoming bigger. This image pattern—the circle with hunger at its core—is mirrored in a second configuration, the web and its weaver or breaker. Again the object stands, simultaneously, for unity and isolation, interconnectedness and entanglement. And at its center is one who joins and cuts—the artist-hero. These two central images structure the complex panorama of *Babel-17*.

The chapters of the novel are disposed in such a way that they form a series of intersecting circles. In a book where people seek to name themselves in order to exist, the chapters present a row of five names: two proper ones, two titles, and in the center a name linked with a place—Jebel Tarik, a possessive which in this language form ("Old Moorish") lacks the possessive inflection. The outer chapters, one and five ("Rydra Wong" and "Marcus T'mwarba"), form a circle which joins poet and scientist, heart and reason, a girl and her stepfather-in-spirit. Things comes full circle and poles connect when Marcus, in the final pages, at last understands the meaning of Rydra's childhood ordeal with the talking mynah bird and the worm. Because he sees how she entered another being, he will be able to enter her. Union is explosion; his old science collapses ("It was a hysterical onset brought about by her previous condition. . . "), but a new one takes its place which permits him to "worm his way" through their telepathic prison. The next layer of chapters as we move inward, "Ver Dorco" and "The Butcher," also forms a family circle: these two are father and son by blood, yet have no affinity but hate, the perversion of natural love. Their union closes not in life, but in death—the son kills his own parent. The central chapter itself forms a miniature circle in which a name is ever chasing its object. The other names are essentially "objectless"; this desire is the force that moves them. Rydra incribes a vast circle in one direction as her ego seeks its complements—lover, muse, and parent. In finding these, she discovers herself: Butcher represents her own criminal nightside. Moving in the other direction, Butcher's arc swings back to the past, probing the reality behind his gruesome *persona*: does the man who doesn't even know the word for "I" have an ego? "Jebel Mountain," on the other hand, would seem a perfect equilibrium between subject and object. Instead of balance, here also is ceaseless circling of opposites: this mountain turns out to be a roving "shadow-ship," its circling mirrored in the dialogue between Rydra and Butcher that takes place in the bowels of Jebel Tarik. As the relationship between "I" and "you" is first reversed, and then righted, the two minds interpenetrate. Yet each finds that, in the glass of this other mind, he is actually chasing himself. Such contact is simultaneously explosive, expansive and contractive—as one circle breaks, another reforms: "I'm a lot bigger than I thought I was, Butcher, and I don't know whether to thank you or damn you for showing me." Rydra will spin in these circles until the pattern is broken by Marcus at the point where the two "great circles," heroine-lover and heroine-parent, meet to form the more stable triad.

The circles in *Babel*, then, do not remain concentrically apart: they overlap, intersecting in a lateral sense. Butcher, for instance, has already killed his father and joined that circle in the second chapter, before he even appears in the novel. Only in the last chapter does he discover his true identity, and thus recognizes his deed. The same circle closes again on a different plane, and only in order to break. For as soon as Butcher can encompass his criminal past, he is free of it. Furthermore, in order for this father-son circle to form, Marcus must connect with Rydra at the juncture of her bird experience. This event also spans the whole novel. First evoked by T'mwarba in chapter one, its meaning eludes him until chapter five. The seminal moment, the point of revelation, comes in the middle, and as the result of yet another circle forming and breaking—Rydra and Butcher. Circles abound in *Babel* on many levels, microcosmic and macrocosmic. But the small may expand, and the large contract: circles interract in this novel like a series of shock waves radiating outward, or imploding. Delany's own images suggest this constant dynamic: "Fling a jewel into a glut of jewels"; "Drop a gem in thick oil."

Babel is full of references to food, the preparation and eating of food, and hunger. This syndrome of imagery intersects the circle pattern itself in the several banquet scenes that occur throughout the novel. There are three moments of collective unity or disunity in these basic human acts of eating. At two extremes are the dinner party at Baron Ver Dorco's, and the dinner on top of the Alliance Towers. In each there is a similar setting of conventional "elegance." Yet one ends in chaos, the other in harmony. In the center—the banquet on Jebel Tarik—the web of human relationships that spans these eating circles is both shattered and refashioned as conspirator and poet face each other. The banquet at Ver Dorco's is a sterile circle of conventions, an empty mockery of social intercourse. The meal itself is prepared by a machine—it is lavish but soulless. Real relationships, however, cannot be excluded from this circle: they intrude both for good and for evil. Rydra's crew is invited out of politeness. Calli's rudeness (he expresses genuine likes and dislikes) both shocks and delights the Baroness—the experience opens her eyes to the absence of true communication beneath the facade of aristocratic civility. Ironically, it is an uninvited guest, the TW-55 superzombie, who permanently disrupts the party by killing the host. He too, before performing his murder, gives Rydra his real opinions: rudeness here is less a matter of convention than intention. Through this agent, it is the son who judges both his parents' society and their own sterile union: they were able to sacrifice him to an empty social vision, a world held together not by love and equality, but difference and war. By a stroke of counter irony, his violent act reunites the Baron and Baroness, if only in death: she falls to the floor cradling the head of her husband—the first display of genuine emotion in all this falseness.

In another way, and to opposite ends, this scenario is repeated during the dinner at the Towers. Once again Rydra's strange crew enters a circle of conventional manners and elegance—this time a restaurant reserved not for aristocrats but high-level bureaucrats. Reverberations here are positive: not only are the crew accepted, but they come to accept as well—the two worlds of Transport and Customs join in the absent center which is Rydra Wong. The opulence of Ver Dorco's table, in its artificiality, is worthy of a Roman orgy. This is a kind of reverse elegance—real food is served here (ironically, hamburger and ketchup have become luxuries). Though the crew's cook is an "artist" with the "carbo-synth," the guests are awed by the real thing—it is so bland and banal that in Delany's relativist perspective it becomes exotic—and accept it willingly. Only at the point where worlds meet in harmony—each side retaining its weaknesses as well as strengths—does Marcus get the information about Rydra that leads to unraveling the Babel-17 mystery. At Ver Dorco's (out of deference to "good manners"), the "discorporate" were not invited: Rydra brought one along anyway as a secret sharer. He was also present during the crucial interchange between Rydra and Butcher. And, fortunately, he was also invited this time, for it is from the mouth of this ghost whom Rydra not only tolerated but befriended that Marcus gets the key to the puzzle.

Central to these banquets and to *Babel* as a whole is hunger. As a force that drives in two directions—to destroy and to create—hunger is behind the two major encounters in the novel: Baron Ver Dorco and Nyles, Rydra and Butcher (again, as with the Rydra-Marcus-Butcher axis, two parallel sets of relationships resolve into a triad, because they share a common term). In *Babel*, hunger is the other face of civilization. As his nickname implies, Butcher is the aristocratic boy literally turned inside out by hunger. The war between Alliance and Invader is a war of embargoes; cities cut off from each other begin to devour themselves. On the individual level, starvation brings cannibalism—both literal and figurative. General Forester remembers being attacked in the streets by scrawny teen-age girls with razors: "Come here beefsteak. Come get me, lunchmeat." All throughout the novel, the same forces on different levels pervert the family and love relationship. To Rydra, Baron Ver Dorco has a cannibal look; he claims to be "starved" for conversation. His aristocratic vision of the world is one of isolation, a web of starved beings whose only possible bond is the desire to devour each other: "Sometimes I believe. . . that without the Invasion, something for the Alliance to focus its energies upon, our society would disintegrate." Ver Dorco's hunger is less physical than intellectual. In its isolation it is totally destructive. The seeker of ideal form is ironically a maker of perfect weapons. In his quest, he "devours" his own son, takes his "I" from him long before Babel-17 enters the picture. This intellectual hunger (in another twist of irony) first reduces Ver Dorco to the animal—he has the smile and teeth of a predator—and finally brings him to eat himself in a quite literal manner. The TW-55 superspy who kills him is more than an extension of his son; through that son, it becomes the projection of his own ravenous desires. As this Shakespeare-quoting zombie ("Yon Cassius has a lean and hungry look") touches Ver Dorco with his vibra-gun, those appetites come their full destructive circle.

Rydra wonders, however, when she speaks with TW-55, just how hungry Ver Dorco really is. At best it is an empty hunger, mirrored in death and the berserk food machine that pours out dishes chaotically, soullessly, as the banquet is disrupted. Against this sterile urge, Rydra's hunger is creative. It will lead less to satiety than to "conception," in a sense that is simultaneously sexual and intellectual—the union of beings in life. Her attraction to Babel-17 is a strangely physical hunger: "When she asked herself that question [who spoke Babel?], her stomach would tighten, her hands start toward something and the yearning for an answer grow nearly to pain in the back of her throat." Butcher is driven by a similar violent hunger to communicate in Babel-17. Groping out from the imperfect language, he pounds his fist to express its missing words. Literally cutting in hopes of joining, he opens the dead pregnant woman and tries to save the embryo: perhaps here is someone to whom he can teach his language. The same aching need makes him "fish up" Rydra's wayward ship, and later attach himself to her, wholly uncritical of her words or actions. On the plane of artistic creation, Rydra's drive to enter another person (Rimbaud's *je est un autre*?) is but a higher form of this same hunger. Ver Dorco's art is lifeless. Not only is the "statue" that descends from this Pygmalion's pedestal a bringer of death—it is the negation of life. We see this clearly in its speech itself, for talk is only an illusion of life. TW-55 speaks in set discourses—a lexicon but not a language. With Babel-17, however, Butcher possesses a language system. The two yearning seekers then meet on this level of system, coming together in what is literally a linguistic sex-act. TW-55 (as Rydra discovers in her fruitless conversation with it before Ver Dorco's assassination) turns in endless word circles. With Butcher the circle of "you" and "I" proves most fertile.

These words explode with meaning: I/Aye/Eye—self, affirmation, perception—to perceive is to change; you/ewe/you—other self, female, death—to change is to follow the cycle of life. But if life itself is change in permanence, the two seekers discover that speech, the act of naming, is freedom: "Central in you I see mirror and motion fused. . . and everything is choice."

Long ago as a child, in her ordeal with the mynah bird and worm, Rydra had discovered the destructive power of hunger. Behind the screen of civilized words (the bird says: "Hello, Rydra, it's a fine day out and I'm happy") lies a carnivorous reality: "The only thing this meant in the bird's mind was a rough combination of . . . sensations that translated loosely—*There's another earthworm coming*." Now she experiences the same nightside on entering Butcher's mind. By going into the bird, Rydra was actually entering herself—*it* was not afraid of the worm, *she* was. In Butcher's mind she understands this. She can do so because, as they mix promiscuously in Butcher's confusion of the personal pronouns, he tells his own worm story. As "I" becomes "you," she again sees through another's eyes. By the same token, however, she can overcome her fear this time, for though Butcher was terrified, he killed his giant worms: "You were scared, but you killed them. . . You killed them, and when you knew you could beat them, you weren't afraid anymore." Seeing herself thus mirrored, she can kill the worm at the core of her own existence. To do so she must realize that darkness lies not in bird or worm, but in herself. She is the traitor in her own ship. In this same mirror, the artist sees herself joined with the "criminal consciousness." The result of this "reverse sexuality" is mutual impregnation. He in the mirror of her person discovers his suppressed light side—"the light you make!"

The other central image is that of the web. If *Babel* is not a novel of action, neither is it a novel of fatality, celebrating the web that binds men together despite their will. To control is to name. Thus the webs in *Babel* are constructs of language; as such, they can either entangle and isolate, or unite. To break this ambiguity of the web, the heroine plunges not into action but into the language system itself. She starts by explosing a web of sabotage, and ends by investigating how webs themselves are made or broken. From macrocosmic promise, the field of *Babel* contracts to a microcosmic center—the speaker or weaver of webs struggling with the paradoxes of communication that hold the key to this varied universe. Indeed, there is a profusion of webs in the novel, woven from the most diverse centers: Ver Dorco's network of a society fused by war, the web of treachery Geoffrey Cord unfolds at the center of the banquet on Jebel Tarik. But if the speaker is all-important, the paradox of Babel-17 is that it is a speakerless language—

it has no word for "I." The transcriptions Rydra gets are dialogue, but in speaking Babel with Butcher she loses her "I" only to gain a bigger sense of self. Ver Dorco, Cord, and Rydra herself before this moment, speak to assert themselves, to cast language nets over others. Because Babel-17 has no egocenter, however, self and other (the "I" and "you") really become "interchangeable." A new web of language is formed whose designation is the pronoun "we": to speak is, simultaneously, to give self to another, and to receive from that other a sense of self larger than before, because it is two. Clever in itself, this could remain word-juggling of the "death once dead" variety, empty conceits and preciosity. But in the dialogue between artist and criminal at the core of his novel, Delany's paradoxes take on flesh and form. The drama that unfolds on this analytical level of system is nonetheless a drama.

Delany's world is clearly fallen. This new language may seem the perfect instrument of communication. In its speakerless perfection, however, this seventeenth variation on Babel, far from reuniting men only divides them further. In pursuit of its patterns, both Rydra and Butcher weave a web of sabotage and death across the galaxies. There is a twist here. As an abstraction, Babel-17 is dangerous precisely because it denies that diversity of language that resulted from the fall of the original tower. The old presumption rises from a new base: "Also, Babel-17 is such an exact analytical language, it almost assures you technical mastery of any situation you look at. And the lack of an "I" blinds you to the fact that though it's a highly useful way to look at things, it's the only way." The quest for the absolute blinds and thus restricts, while acceptance of limits—the fact that the speech act is necessarily relative, that any utterance implies a specific "point of view"—leads to expansion. Delany's is a fortunate fall, for the necessary condition for unity in this world seems to be the broadest possible diversity—Babelian variety itself. In this novel true union of human beings occurs only where speech centers are most disparate; communication is most creative when tension between the speakers is at a maximum. Each man, in fact, weaves his own language web. To the extent that he knows himself, each is potentially an artist. Ver Dorco seeks only perfection, control through his art; instead, he finds death. Rydra too at the outset is fascinated with the power Babel-17 bestows—but control again brings isolation, and even death. As maker and breaker of webs, she is also caught in this futile pattern. To break it she must "name" herself. The trap is sprung by love: her union with Butcher at the nexus of love and hate (should she thank or curse him?) leads each to realize his "I" in the fullest sense, to channel its limits, its dynamic instability, to creative ends. The abstract triad of *Towers* (perfection-death-transition) is altered in a way which prefigures the eminently human pattern of *The Einstein Intersection*: death-art-love.

Rydra's quest is essentially one of growth as an artist. She passes from assertion of special "talent" or genius to acceptance of her common humanity. In the latter, paradoxically, she finds her true uniqueness—that "I" which leads to the expanded artistic vision, to a more effective power of action. Rydra possesses from the start a web-like sensory apparatus, "an antenna of several thousand miles surface area." What she will later realize is that her "telepathy" is a matter of fine tuning only: each human nervous system has this potential. She learns that, instead of merely "jamming" these webs, or covering and completing them, her task as artist is to stimulate them to develop and reach out. At the outset, Rydra's "telepathy" is acute but significantly limited in scope. She "reads" Forester's gestures, not his mind. When she chooses her pilot, she performs another feat of reading body-language. Though she knows nothing about pilots, she observes the physical reactions of one who does, Ron the Navigator, as he watches Brass wrestle. Pilots must literally wrestle their ship through hyperspace. In the muscular empathy between these two, Rydra senses this one's finesse. But if Ron and Brass are in harmony, she remains an outsider. Her view of poetry marks her position at this point. Awkward feelers like those of Forester, reaching to communicate, "hurt" her; so she "polishes" and finishes these emotional patterns in her poems to stop the pain. This one-sided action is a perfection that isolates rather than joins—Forester remains painfully alone.

More than a maker of webs that exclude, Rydra on Jebel Tarik becomes a breaker of webs. The way to a genuinely constructive art must lead through the realization of its very real destructive power. Babel-17, like Lobey's "ax" and Mouse's syrinx in *Nova*, becomes a weapon. Rydra's pursuit of the mysterious language leads her first to shatter the web of bandages, then that of the Invader spaceships: "It was not only a language. . . but a flexible matrix of analytical possibilities where the same "word" defined the stresses in a webbing of medical bandage, or a defensive grid of spaceships. What would it do with the tensions and yearnings in a human face?" In the banquet scene, Rydra has what is perhaps her first real telepathic experience: she hears minds making voices, "braiding with one another." Into this a false note impinges with murderous dissonance—the ironically (and punningly) named Cord. She encompasses his web of tortured ambition. Unable to let him destroy the web she is weaving as she pursues the Babel tapes, she casts her net of contorted poetry over his own in a striking recitation scene, and he "snaps." Telepathy here has become (she realizes) the nexus of the old talent and a new way of thinking—Babel-17. When the harmony of her mental construct—her Babelian "wordview"—is invaded, she turns her art to crush the invader. What she does not yet realize, however, is that this "wordview" is a destructive one—she herself is the saboteur she seeks. But if here she creates to destroy, in her subsequent union with Butcher she is destroyed in order to be created. For the first time she invades another mind, and is annihilated: she sees her own image, just as if a mirror had been hurled into her face. This destruction leads to the rebirth of both person and artist. As the two minds fuse in this "telepathic union," they invert—she becomes the criminal, he the artist. If one common language joins them, it will separate them as well. This time a web of language is thrown over them which isolates in order to make whole. A maze of paradoxes is run through these minds held by the subjectless Babel, forcing each to "escape" back to the other side of his brain. Reversing Cord's fatal rupture, Butcher's neck "cracks" as he snaps back to his original identity. Each recovers the dynamic duality that must lie at the heart of the language process—the fortunate split between subject and object that provides the only base upon which to rebuild Babel—the "self-critical process." One of the painful consequences of the fall is that there is no longer any necessary connection between words and objects, between reality and our representation of it; but in this split lies hope for our salvation as well. The symbol may control the chimpanzee (red *is* stop), but man, by knowing himself as namer of things, can in turn control his symbols. Rydra reveals her new-found knowledge of this "symbolic process" by cracking the web of war itself. She overloads the circuits, to complete rather than destroy: she introduces the "missing element" in this language—peace. When the word-mirror of her identical sentences is thrown in these respective faces, each will "escape" toward the common center of humanity. Rydra calls this her "best prose sentence." To accomodate her new vision, she may have to abandon lyric forms for something larger and more linguistically complex: "I'm going to write a poem, I think. But it may be a novel. I have a lot to say."

The Einstein Intersection (1967) is short, but still a work of extreme complexity and resonance. Like *Babel*, it is tightly patterned; yet, in its greater suggestive power, its structures resist analysis, forcing the reader to "bite through the shells" of their meanings. *Einstein* also approaches the human condition on the level of system; but it goes somewhat deeper. In *Babel*, man's fate remains essentially a linguistic and grammatical problem. The paradox of the fall is mirrored in the paradox of language itself: though each man is (potentially) a separate speech-world, this bewildering variety of tongues leads not to isolation but to its opposite—the hunger of the worm in Eden resembles that of these island-men in their attempt to communicate with each other. *Einstein* deals with the fall in terms of an analagous system: myth. Not only is there a similar profusion and confusion of myths, but they too are seen essentially as language constructs: verbal scenarios for human action sanctioned by tradition or authority. Delany's sense of the language act, in this novel, has a broader social valence.

Einstein embraces a view of the fall reminiscent of Rousseau's in his *Discourse on the Origins of Inequality*. To Rousseau the fall is simultaneously a speech act and a social choice: "The first man who fenced off a piece of land and said: *This is mine,* and who found people simple-minded enough to take him at his word, was the true originator of society." *Einstein* is less about myth than about this process of myth-making. Lobey, as he cuts through the diverse "wordviews" that generate and maintain social bonds in his world, confronts myth less as form than as dynamic system. Inequality, "difference," is the central theme of this novel. Motivated by his own sense of being "different," Lobey's quest lays bare this supremely human process of building fences, evoking mythic patterns in order to separate individuals from each other and from nature. Rydra controls the larger world by naming herself. In *Einstein*, we encounter a series of namers who control by keeping others from naming themselves. "The labyrinth today does not follow the same path it did at Knossos fifty thousand years ago," Lobey is told. Indeed, his maze *is* different—instead of concrete reality, he faces language systems, potentiality. He too seeks to "name himself"—to define his place in the world, to grasp the meaning of his actions. But the patterns offered him are partial and inadequate—from the "lo" particle to the contradictory mythical archetypes he meets with. If he finds illusion, it is only partly a mirror of self (he does pursue his selfish love for Friza, only to discover hate-in-love: the outraged lover stabs Greeneye as he hangs on the "tree"). Illusion in *Einstein* is also a mirror projected by others for selfish ends: the Dove's *Pearl*, Spider's institutionalized disorder. Because of this dimension—closer to purposeful "evil"—this book projects a wider vision of the human condition than *Babel*. As Rydra and Butcher interpenetrate, the darkside of man is named. If it is not abolished, at least it is accepted as an element in the human dynamic—creative as well as destructive. But in the final pages of *Einstein* Lobey faces Spider. Where the former remains confused—there is relation between destruction and construction, but what is it?—the latter affirms his power to manipulate these polar categories to personal advantage.

On one hand, Lobey's journey from forest to town appears to retrace Rousseau's fall. On the other, however, it seems a quest for life renewal, through the waste land to the waters of regeneration. An extract from the "Author's Journal" placed at the head of one of the unnumbered chapters describes the composition of *Einstein* as the overlaying of lines or "filagrees" on a palimpsest. To superimpose such patterns of significance is to suspend their contradictory or antinomian natures. It is at this level—heroic action as a system of possibilities—that Delany introduces his protagonist/narrator. Lobey confronts his world at a particular point of stress—the paradox of "difference." He meets with endless linguistic and logical divisions, physical and social inequalities. Yet here as in *Babel* (but on a broader scale), chaos is the necessary precondition for order—to differentiate is also to classify, to arrange, even to shape. At least in its aspirations, Lobey's quest as fallen-man is more concrete and fundamental than Rydra's—he would overcome death. His problems begin as his goal is overlayed with myth, as he encounters Kid Death. For Lobey the fall is less "fortunate," the outcome of his adventure more inconclusive. In Rydra, light and darkness join; because she sees this she in turn links galaxies. But if, in like manner, Lobey at the end sees in himself both the power of life and death ("Like the Kid I can bring back the ones I've killed myself"), he is never sure whom he has killed, or what he has chosen. By the physical fact of his quest—sheer movement—Lobey links worlds, and causes basic patterns to form. He experiences things and even chronicles them. But it is the "Author" who speaks of palimpsest. The degree to which Lobey understands the processes of his world or his art (let alone controls them) remains unclear.

But can we speak of human patterns if *Einstein* is the story of non-human "psychic manifestations" who seek to inhabit a world ostensibly abandoned by men? The alien who adopts man's systems becomes human himself, and this is exactly what happens to these beings. Delany approaches things from this perspective in order to redefine what is human; instead of physical norms and mythified codes of conduct, there emerges a basic rhythm of existence. In his discussion of the Einstein intersection, Spider describes this rhythm. As he displaces these intersecting explanations of man's relationship to his physical universe into the moral sphere, he himself ironically becomes an example of this dynamic at work. The explicator tries to dominate his model. Though he sees the rhythmic interplay of the two laws—concave to convex curve—he yearns to give them a diachronic relationship: the Goedelian line "eagles over" that of Einstein; a new reign has begun. Nevertheless, this Goedelian prophet is still in an Einsteinian situation: his perception is necessarily limited by his condition. All the figures in this novel have precise conditions, social or otherwise. As soon as they seek to erect their partial visions into closed systems, they encounter the Goedlian situation: "In any closed. . . system there are an infinite number of true theorems which, though contained in the original system, cannot be deduced from it." To establish limits is simultaneously to deny them. Each character finds himself at every minute at this Einstein intersection. In approaching humanity at this level of system, Delany turns the traditional novel of initiation and quest upside down, freeing his narrative from the tyranny of a "realism" that itself is but another myth. In this world of dynamic bipolarities, there is constant "slippage" between coordinates: Lobey can be both Orpheus and Ringo, singer and silent, both or neither. If quest at this level cuts through "irreconcilable" opposites—exposing them as codes or conventions—its goal is not realism but reality itself. Lobey's basic hunger—to save Friza and kill Kid Death—is (if unconsciously) a search for more permanent patterns—the perfection of threes. Like Rydra, he begins as the sole survivor of a broken "triple." But if she at the end of her novel finds a momentary tripartite union with Marcus and Butcher, Lobey ends as he started—alone. Along the way, however, he encounters (if only in potentiality) the triad. What is more important, as he passes through this world, he articulates it into patterns of three. If the hero remains on the Einsteinian edge ("which did I choose?") his journey is a linear fact that has forced stable contours to emerge in this seemingly chaotic world. These patterns, we discover, are both familiar and eminently human.

The basic facts in the world of *Einstein* are radiation and mutation. Man has either destroyed himself or abandoned a destroyed planet. In the rebuilding process, these alternatives become as irrelevant as the absence of man. The facts simply introduce randomness; these beings cope with it in very human ways. On his trek from forest to sea, Lobey encounters three distinct societies defined by place: village, tribe, and town. He passes from his traditional village society with its strict sense of "norms" and prescribed rites of initiation; through the anarchistic society of the dragon herders where the only norm is survival, the only ritual the bond of physical hunger; to the "town," a sprawling metropolis with social codes based on family influence and economic power. The existence of a possible fourth place—the "city"—is significant. These builders, paradoxically, have not attained this level, and yet have surpassed it. The ruined "city" with its central axis possesses an order Branning-at-Sea does not have. But Branning's name belies its reality—instead of a sleepy resort, we have the familiar modern city growing at random. The ancient ruin, with its "main street," seems more like the town. Names then are problematical. And being "human" is more than following some traditional blueprint or formulated line of development. The axis upon which these social systems are built is not found on the ground. They exist primarily in the mind at that intersection where limits themselves form and dissolve:

they are generative models. As these "psychic" entities strive to shape matter, we again (as in *Babel*) grasp the fall at the level of system—separation is the condition that generates dynamic activity. It is less the forms of *Einstein* than the rhythms that are human: organize/separate. In unfamiliar sequence and strange shapes, this dynamic leads to reenactment of patterns that are quite familiar.

Across the landscape of this novel, the Einstein intersection invariably falls at the idea of "difference." In each of the three worlds the word means something different. Each mode of difference in turn produces one individual who is different—a misfit. In terms of his forest world, with its norms and gender distinctions, "Lo" Lobey stands apart as a rebel. In his romantic strivings, he cannot accept its strictures; he is told to "grow up." This society attempts through controls to become human. Where "non-functionals" at first were killed, now they are separated in "kages." Ironically, this tolerance, with its refinement of distinctions, leads not to order but greater confusion. Lo Hawk, who sees the essence of humanity as speech, would rather give the "lo" title to a talking dog than to the silent Friza. For Lobey, however, she communicated with things on a deeper level, creating a web of harmony around her. This system encompasses deceit as well as uncertainty. Lobey is surprised at Dorik's "le"; to him the androgyne has been a "la," to Friza a "lo." From these unions come three children, one Friza's, one Lobey's, and one all Dorik's. This unstable triple (one child is non-functional) mirrors that formed by these three beings, representatives of the three genders. Their union is one of both deception and ignorance of self, and is doubly precarious as a result. Each is "different" in that he possesses telepathic powers. But these are potentially as destructive as they are constructive. Friza can throw rocks as well as protect against them. And Lobey makes music by taking it from others' minds. But only by seeing the extent to which his art can be a weapon—a stifler of minds rather than a force that joins them—will he learn to use it constructively, to bring back those he has killed.

The desert world of nomads and "outlaws" recognizes no gender distinctions. The only law or order is survival. Behind it lies something like chance: inexplicably, some thrive, while others do not. The only test of "functionality" is pragmatic. Kid Death is both the product of this ethic and its reject. In the desert the "kage" is more an extermination camp. Whereas elders seek to guide Lobey, Kid's father would suppress him. A "redheaded blond with gills," Kid is totally unadapted to his world, yet survives through another compensating "difference"—like Friza he has the power of teleportation. His talent too is ambiguous—with it he can both take life and give it. First he uses it to bring water, to save others; then he kills with it. This destruction ironically isolates him, for now he must seek water, and live immersed in the sea.

In the desert, "difference" is a law of nature; in Branning, as in the forest, it is a social law. Each of the latter legislates to contrary ends. Behind Branning's codes and distinctions, there is not respect for some traditional ideal of "humanity," but sheer drive for power and social status. In the city there are two modes of difference: the concealed economic disparity between rulers and subjects, and an illusory sense of "difference" foisted on the masses by tricks and advertising campaigns. Slogans delude: "These two identical twins are not the same"—sameness is difference. In like manner, one figure, the Dove, is all things to all people—each sexual fantasy appears to be unique and different, yet its source is always the same. Significantly, the "kage" here is no more than a mirror image of the normal world—a hellish "floor show" that literally reflects the hell of illusion above. Compared with the varied articulations of the village, the music Lobey senses in Branning is droning monotony—all qualitative distinctions have been dissolved in an endless quantitative mixing: "Though ten are nice, ninety-nine. . . are *so* much nicer!" When Lobey appears to find Friza again in Dove, the dark beauty in the blonde, the earlier broken triad with Dorik seems to reform. Again the third element turns out to be androgynous—this time, however, the delusion is both grotesque and inhuman. As "eternal feminine," Dove is barren; and where Dorik at least had physical reality, Dove and the Friza "she" invokes are no more than sterile mirror images, all differences dissolve. In spite of this, though, there *are* differences in Branning. The "lo" and "la" designations have become titles of nobility here, reserved for "four or five" big families. When Lobey would use his "lo," he is told to "keep his differences to himself." In the forest these particles are used for genetic classification. Here genetics itself has become a levelling process, the means of "keeping confusion in the trails-fertile," of assuring control by the few over the many. In this world too difference is a means of survival: "I'm very talented, Lobey, in what I do," Dove tells him, "I've had to perfect that talent to survive. You can't ignore the laws of the world you've chosen." In contrast to this artistic conformity is Greeneye, the creator whose very birth (as with Kid) makes him an outcast. His parthenogenesis ironically is a menace to the genetic hegemony of his conservative ruling family.

Inequality in *Einstein* is a natural as well as a social fact. Out of it seems to come the hope of new unity. Each of the three misfits are alike both in their telepathic powers and (if to varying degrees) in their lack of parents. But just as Lobey is given limited counsel by the village elders, all of these orphans find parent figures in this world, and through them plunge into new inequality. The careers of each are spanned by two such parents in particular: PHAEDRA the computer and Spider, mother and father. Indeed, if this triad possesses potential harmony only, more dynamic in the breakdown of its configurations than in its unity, it is because these authority figures create ties that destroy rather than bind. Both are tentacular forms, both purveyors of difference, but from opposite angles. The computer is a detached cynic, an aesthete; Spider is a repressive tyrant. One offers uncreative chaos, the other beings destructive order.

PHAEDRA assumes the cynical voice of a long-dead "humanity." This blase machine is the repository for a jumble of disembodied myths and traditional patterns. Soulless itself, it is a mockery of the role of sage or elder. Yet this is exactly what it professes to be in its hip-talking condescension: "Mankind had style, baby! You may get it yet, but right now your charm is a very young thing." "She" not only belittles Lobey's quest ("Mother is in charge. . . Scoot!") but taunts it with an alternate maze of myths. In the cave the computer plays Phaedra to his Theseus and the mutant-minotaur. Later in Branning "she" appears again, this time as Minos himself, but a different version, a travesty of Dante's Keeper of Hell, accompanied by a "talking dog" who (as a grotesque reflection of Hawk's earlier remark) plays to her role a fatuous Cerberus: "Lo Lobey! Have you been enjoying the floor show her at *The Pearl*!" PHAEDRA is both a mythomaniac (Psychic Harmony Entanglements and Deranged Response Association ironically becomes PHAEDRA) and a connoisseur of difference. For "her," however, myth is no more than a suave illusion, powerless to shape or guide. She can tantalize Lobey in the labyrinth—offer to play his Ariadne—or pass aesthetic judgment on his actions: "I'd love to see you work with a muleta. Ole!" But she is helpless to lead him: "You're in the wrong maze. . . and I'm the wrong girl to get you into the right one." Behind this sequence of roles is chaos.

Spider is as grave and moralizing as PHAEDRA is flippant. Behind his lessons and theorizing lies an even greater danger to these seekers: instead of the machine's self-centeredness, here is the powerful citizen driven by self-interest. This expounder of the Einstein intersection is in reality a kind of Goedelian messiah: "Something new is happening to the fragments [of man's abandoned world], something we can't even define with mankind's leftover vocabulary. You must take its importance exactly as that: it is undefinable. . . it is wonderful, fearful, deep. . . yet it demands you take journeys, defines your stopping and starting points. . . " It is not that this vision is contradictory so much as that it sanctions contradiction, wields irrationality as an instrument of power. Spider plots his moral landscape in similar terms: "I'm Greeneye's Iscariot. I'm Kid Death's Pat Garrett. . . I'm every traitor you've imagined. And I'm a baron of dragons, trying to support two wives and ten children.'' Lobey calls him a ''big man;'' and indeed he is ruler of this world. His concern over Green-eye is both collective and conservative: ''all of us may be hurt.'' More a Pilate than an Iscariot, he signs his death warrant to preserve a status-quo which lies (it turns out) in ''riots'' and contrived confusion. Spider poses as a liberator: he ''frees'' Kid from his father, and Lobey from his selfish view of ''difference,'' his narrow sense of the quest. What he really does, however, is to weave his web of destruction. Kid Death is already ''tied up'' by ''their past''—by the curiosity and fear he experieces through other's eyes as, from his underwater ''kage,'' he opens and closes them. By killing Kid's father, Spider ''unties'' him only to indebt him, ensnaring him further. Later he takes him in a deadlier net—as Lobey's music transfixes him, Spider kills him with his whip.

He would do the same with Lobey—free him of one view of reality in order to bind him in another. Dorik had claimed that Lobey, in his sense of difference, refused to accept the ''real world.'' Spider tells him much the same thing: ''You're living in the real world now. . . It's come from something. It's going to something.'' But where Dorik saw change circumscribed by ''right and wrong,'' Spider sees unbounded randomness: ''Myths always lie in the most difficult places to ignore. They confound all family love and hate.'' In the name of this sole value of family, Spider later leads Lobey to see his myth-guided quest in an irrational light: ''If I reach Friza, I don't know what I'll have, even if I get her.'' At the same time, he would tie him to Green-eye and Kid Death by creating a web of mutual interdependencies (''Kid. . . can control, but he cannot order. And that is why he needs you''). Spider later manipulates this web when he has Lobey hold Kid's mind with his music while he kills him. The vision of this apostle of ''difference'' is both a chaotic one that refuses rational categories (a town simply ''grows bigger'' until it becomes a city), and an interested one that makes irrationality the tool of tyranny. His reinterpretation of the ''source cave'' is an example. For the long-vanished men, this was apparently a radiation shelter. The elders of the village have turned this around: the cave has become the source of myth and life—it is the place of Lobey's rite of passage. To Spider, however, it is this: ''the lower levels contain the source of the radiation by which the villages, when their populations become too stagnant, can set up a controlled random jumbling of genes and chromosomes.'' Lobey's village sought to control the random. Spider's world controls randomness, keeping the genes mixing so as to level and confound, to preserve the barons' lines. It takes parthenogenesis to disturb these.

A curious thing about this novel is that everything is different and yet somehow familiar. The events *do* follow the usual patterns: Kid Death is betrayed, Lobey loses Friza, Green-eye is crucified. Different myths may be jumbled and superimposed, but each in itself comes true. Delany's own patterns are also ubiquituous. Spider is a triple man—he herds dragons, writes, plays music. He posits a triad of imperatives—change, order, create. The texture of *Einstein*, again, is formed of decomposing threes and yearning, "hungry" ones. Two of the three misfits have visibly split existences, the sort seen in *Babel.* Kid Death is a solipsist who would draw all to himself—and yet he is constantly reaching out for a friend. If Green-eye refuses his advances, Spider accepts them only to betray (Kid dies crying: "you're supposed to be my friend"). What kills Kid is a "need" for music. This strange Death figure can destroy by absorbing others in his private "kage," and yet tempt Green-eye with the most constructive vision in the novel—that of Earth rebuilding in three balanced sectors: "Star-probe. . . depth gauge. . . rock drill." In like manner, Lobey's music orders and destroys: his "ax" is both instrument and weapon. He spears Kid just as surely with his music as he sticks Green-eye with the blade. Again a triad forms and dissipates.

These half beings are held apart by Spider's divisive vision. This latter says Kid Death can control but not order. Not only does Kid's vision in the desert prove him wrong, but his very idea of death is an ordering of life. In Lobey's village La Dire has said: "all life is a rhythm, all death is rhythm suspended." This is how Kid kills—he closes eyes and opens them, takes and brings back. Lobey as musician is said to order, not control. In reality he does both. Not only does he take music from minds to perfect or polish it, he forces it on them as well. Like Dionysos, he sways the crowd at *The Pearl*, he "makes the music make them." All these undulations, however, like La Dire's vision, are fundamentally monistic—they are tautologies. Lobey drops, and is retrieved by Kid in the "broken land"; but it is not this rhythm, we discover, that brings him back to life. The same is true with Lobey: his music cannot resurrect Friza, but merely moves shades of illusion, Dove as Friza. The only thing that breaks these tautologies is Green-eye's power to "create." He can bring Friza back because he "creates something from nothing"—he offers a genuine duality, the possibility of differentiation. As Butcher does for Rydra, he provides that other entity, the mirror flung in the face and smashed; this leads the half-being to discover his whole self as a dynamic union of opposites. In the key central scene in the "broken land," Green-eye appears in Lobey's mind. In physical terms the latter has merely swooned and recovered. Inside his mind, however, Green-eye can show him how he has died: "You just gave up. . . and you let the heart stop and the brain blank!" This outside perspective is needed to show Lobey how he has died: "You just gave up. . . and you let the heart stop and the brain blank!" This outside perspective is needed to show him that primarily he controls his life, not another. If Kid can bring back those he kills, Lobey will make this same claim in the end—he admits at least the possibility that he is responsible for his acts.

The world of *Einstein* remains for those who must live it, at most, one of possibility. In their comings and goings, these figures continually miss each other, remaining isolated in their inability to grasp the complex patterns of the whole. None of them (as with Rydra and Butcher) is ever really able to name self in the other. Green-eye designates his creative power by the term "love." Yet love seems basically reflexive here. As Lobey dangles in the "broken land," and the shade of Friza tries to save him, he looks in the mirror of his love only to see himself: "I hurt and loved her, held on and didn't fall." Knowing Kid Death will break the line, he hangs on, saves himself, and the image conjured is shattered. Earlier (ironically), Lobey "permutated" Green-eye's words: "There is no death, only love," into the selfishness of his quest for Friza. Entering Lobey's mind, Green-eye names his solipsistic existence: "You're dead, Lobey!" Yet apparently he cannot perceive his own death—like the being, his maxim is one-eyed. He goes blindly to his gruesome end in the mirror of the crowd's "love" for him. And when Lobey plays beneath the tree in hopes of resurrecting him, he fails because his art (in its "love") remains the self-conscious image of its maker. He plays for himself.

Asked in the end what his choice was—"between the real and. . . the rest"—Lobey can't answer. Like his world, he too doesn't know where he came from, where he is going. Spider asks him who he is: "I'm. . . Lobey?" He says he is also Orpheus and Ringo the Beatle who didn't sing—a circle of opposites closes on him. In like manner, his final course of action is both open and shut. He "might go" to the outer planets. According to Spider, however, this leads nowhere either: "I did that once. It was all waiting for me when I got back." Out there things may be "different," but the path is always the same. Nevertheless, in spite of his confusion and apparent powerlessness, Lobey has chosen. His choice is less intellectual or moral than physical. *Einstein* ends thus: "As morning branded the sea, darkness fell away at the far side of the beach. I turned to follow it." Rydra found darkness, and herself, in Butcher's mind. Lobey is still lost, still pursuing it alone—but he pursues. The difference between light and dark is (at least) clearly drawn here, firmly linked to the rhythm of nature. And throughout the novel the physical fact of Lobey's journey alone has forced differences to be made. Dove, whose talent is the breaking of links, is driven by Lobey to make an important one: ''We live on their planet *because* they destroyed it.'' And PHAEDRA, ''herself,'' a futile gallery of mirrors, is made to exclaim: ''Turn again, Lobey. Seek somewhere outside the frame of the mirror.'' This hero who ''begs at the tree'' may remain throughout a captive of the mirrors of self and world, yet his quest has met with the most tangible reality—the bull magnificent in his death, the hunger and satiety of the dragon herder's meal, Friza's physical struggle to rescue him in the ''broken land.'' Lobey then has no moment of ''recognition,'' tragic or otherwise. Yet his adventure, in forcing distinctions, has laid a base of differentiation, and in doing so opens it to explication as system. It is on this plane that this strange world becomes strangely ours.

Lobey makes his final division of light and darkness, not as hero but as artist. It is he who narrates his story. But what kind of a namer is this being who cannot name himself? Rydra will write her novel only after she solves the mysteries of Babel and self. Lobey approaches the act of narration like he does the world, differently, in a manner Spider calls Goedelian: 'I don't want to know what's inside the myths. . . their limits and genesis. I want their shape, their texture, how they feel when you brush by them on a dark road. . . their weight as they leap your shoulder from behind.'' To Lobey's music Green-eye ''brings words'': he becomes an improviser on the level of prose narration. In the colloquial ''swing'' of his verbal accents, he renders the immediate shapes and textures of experience. But what of the Einsteinian dimension, the limits that necessarily come when the artist chooses a given form, a specific tradition? Lobey's linear improvisation is overlayed, in the epigraphs to these purposely unnumbered ''chapters,'' by an ''author's journal.'' Like an inverted mirror, this tale of the novel's progress covers the actual novel in progress. In the ''journal,'' however, we find the same apparent lack of connection between Goedelian and Einsteinian elements: on one hand, there is directly experienced physical rality, unshaped immediacy (the author on his European tour, cold stones on bare feet); on the other, there are general pronouncements on the novel form—''endings to be useful most be inconclusive.'' Literary tradition seems to offer no mediation. Its various modes and genres are broken into a series of random passages, placed as epigraphs to be experienced in Goedelian fashion, sensual surfaces rather than formal prescriptions. What Delany is giving us in this SF ''novel'' is actually an anatomy of the literary process itself in out times. He presents us here with a literary Babel. Once again dissolution, this time cultural, proves a linguistic concern, and most fortunate. Before there can be new modes of fiction, literary discourse itself must first be cut loose from the various (conflicting) codes that still govern it. *Einstein* performs this deconstruction—but what is rebuilt? Lobey's art is only a dawning. His occasional flourishes are an awkward attempt at "style"; haphazardly he addresses a "you," revealing a primitive sense of an audience. However provocative, *Einstein* remains (in the structuralist sense) a novel of potentiality: it separates more than it remakes. Moving parallel to the narrative present, but not touching it, are the traditional past and the future promise of form.

To a greater degree, that promise is fulfilled in *Nova* (1967). Here too is mythical adventure narrated on a "structural" level, a novel aware of itself as literary process and system. In this work, however, Delany broadens both the sweep of action and the structural coordinates themselves. *Nova* has a genuine diachronic axis, a historical dimension. Past and future provide not only a theoretical but a dynamic, evolutionary frame for the present moment. In the perpetual "now" of *Einstein* the hero lives an essentially synchronic existence, perched on the edge of chaos and order. Lobey journeys from Hawk's "Einsteinian" to Spider's "Goedelian" vision, only to learn that both mentors alike have travelled the same circle to the stars and back. If actions in *Nova* also prove to be circular, they still have a very real linear thrust. Lobey may "deal with" randomness by seeking his name, but the landscape he moves through is (at each and any moment) an ahistorical one of possible names and multiple identities. *Nova* is different: the coordinates now are history and system themselves, the intersection falling on individual man in a new position. In earlier novels, to control the world one first had to name himself. Here, on this historical axis, names take on a life of their own: they are hollow masks dropped in the stream of time, the focus of change. A name is worn by a succession of individuals or peoples who discover their own identity in the process of living the one they have inherited. The central question of *Nova* is: what's in a name? The name of Von Ray has thrown its ambiguous shadow across men's destinies. Saviors to the federation of suns they founded, to their adversaries they are devils. "Criminal, thief, pirate!" At his costume party on "Draco, Earth, Paris, 3162" (each event in *Nova* is thus precisely located), Prince Red gives Lorq Von Ray a pirate's mask. The intergalactic sportsman takes up this gauntlet. Along with his scar (that other, mythical "mask"), he wears this epithet to the end. As hero, Lorq seeks the meaning of his name by asserting its power to change—*ciel ou enfer, qu'importe*. Time alone has operated in the case of Ashton Clark. Because it appeared at the right technological moment, this man's theory changed the world, and his name came to signify change itself: "Ashton Clark to you." To some, however, this name is a blessing, while to others (Mouse's Gypsies, the Vega Republic, for whom this vocational mobility meant cultural dissolution) it is a curse. Lorq gives to the potentiality of his name volition and direction. He will discover that the mask is both hollow and real, that a name both predestines and does not. He alters the balance of the galaxies only to discover the enduring nature of that balance. His far-flung quest to transcend name and meaning leads back to the place in time where both he and his goal were named—New Brazillia with its Illyrion mines, and memories of childhood rivalry with Prince and Ruby. His ship the *Roc* turns out to be a phoenix instead—an extinct literary form, the novel, rises from the flames of this nova. His pursuit of names leads this epic figure beyond the realm of private vengeance and political power. Lorq's quest is keyed throughout at a different level of tension—that between historical man and the various trans-historical patterns that encompass him. Man's fate here unfolds less as a condition—a thing endured—than as a system, something that demands, beyond individual suffering and loss, simply to be understood.

Nova presents us with a Moby Dick situation. A monomaniac captain drives his microcosmic crew into realms where "all law has broken down." Like Ahab's, Lorq's quest is simultaneously universal and personal. During the Tarot reading the first card he draws is the *Kosmos*: "The first card picked always yourself is. But the *Kosmos* a card of the Major Arcana is. A human being it can't represent." Lorq chooses this card, even though his choice limits the possibilities of his future. In confronting the world on this level of "primal cosmic entities," he defies the laws of probability themselves: "What sort of race would it be if I knew I was going to win?" As focus for possible modes of action—mythical, political, natural; the quest for fire, for empire, for the improbable element Illyrion—Lorq pushes on all fronts beyond accepted limits to the inchoate heart of things. He voyages, however, only to find at this center the chaos of his own personal life: at the core of the sun is Ruby's ruined face. Personal needs, love and vengeance, drive him as they drive Ahab—but they push him farther. Only in the meaninglessness of their deaths can he find significance ("I told her once that we had not been fit for meaning. Neither for meaningful deaths"). Only in the terrible paradoxes of existence ("I am free and evil. . . mourning her with my laughter") does he recover a sense of dynamic balance, discover human existence as system. Ahab drags his crew to destruction. In *Nova* there is compensatory balance. There are two ships, two triads with Lorq at the apex—the hero is the term common to both. As Prince and Ruby die, Katin and Mouse are reborn. These hollow lives must perish so that others can invest them with meaning: "Mouse, Katin, you who can speak out of the net, which one of you is the blinder for not having watched me win under this sun?"

Katin indeed is blinded, looks into the nova, only to see. And Lorq both wins and loses. Like Coleridge's Ancient Mariner he survives as life-in-death, the conquered sun now burning inside his frazzled mind, his seven tons of Illyrion no more than one empty hand grabbing the other. On this edge of destruction and reconstruction, nova and novel, we experience something beyond personal tragedy or Faustian defiance—collective humanity functioning at the intersection of history and nature.

Each of the natural systems in *Nova* closes in man. Early in the work the intellectual Katin, dictating a fragment of his "novel in progress," delineates three: the human brain, the interplanetary net of societies, the molecular web of a star or sun. If we cut through any one, we find a core that can balance or deregulate. Inside the brain there is "a nerve cluster that resembles a human figure only centimeters high." But at the heart of these other networks is man also. Three analagous systems run along the diachronic axis in *Nova*, intersecting with the trans-historical at what are essentially human junctures. These are the disciplines of history, social science and physical science—the attempts of men in evolution to deal systematically with change. What Katin calls "history" is the temporal relation of man to events. He distinguishes three successive modes of interpretation: documented tradition, cyclical theory, and the current "integral history." Tradition looks back; cycles in their predictive pretensions look forward. Katin claims the now: "That's my theory. Each individual is a junction in the net, and the strands between are the cultural, the economic, the psychological threads that hold individual to individual. Any historical event is like a ripple in the net." As novelist, however, he cannot so easily transcend time and change. He must go backwards for his form, forward for his audience. He cannot explain this modern theory of history to Idas and Lynceos. Twins who are also opposites, their antiphonal presence disperses as it unites: "Maybe later—", "in the future—", "it'll be easier." There is the same diachronic sequence on the plane of social system—the temporal relation of men to their culture. Again we have three stages: alienation of man from work; Ashton Clark and the "sockets," men directly plugged in to their jobs; present search for "cultural stability" in a world of effortless mobility. Again the focus of this process is a man and instability. Mouse the Gypsy, in his reactionary refusal of "sockets," becomes for Katin (paradoxically) the embodiment of a new union of cultures in chaos: "You've collected the ornamentations a dozen societies have left us over the ages and made them inchoately yours. You're the product of tensions that clashed in the time of Clark and you resolve them on your syrynx with patterns eminently of the present—" Mouse may resolve the past in the improvised present of his art. Yet both his relation to that past and his significance for the future will be given him by Katin: "I've been hunting a subject for my book with both historical import and humanity as well. You're it, Mouse." Here is a different web, with broader crossroads. Lorq is center of the third system—the relation of man to physical nature. The evolution of scientific theory is mirrored in the table of elements itself: Einsteinian rationality, Goedelian breakdown, this in turn superceded by the new "synthetic, integrative" sciences. In like manner, there are stable elements, unstable ones after 98, a return to stability in the "trans-three-hundred elements." In this series as in the others, however, the third term is enigmatic and paradoxical. The rare element Lorq seeks, Illyrion, is both "psychomorphic" and "heterotropic." At the heart of this new stability is something "other," "tending to change." And the root of change is in the mind of man itself. "Illyrion is many things to many people." The key question then is Katin's: "I wonder what it is to our captain."

There is symmetry here—a triad of "heroes" and systems—yet it confers little stability to the surface of *Nova*. Instead, there is an intricate series of displacements. Katin searches for his future in the past, and discovers the physical present. Mouse would flee his past in the present, and is given (in Katin's novel) a future instead. Lorq seeks to live in the "heterotropic" now, but cannot in this manner escape from past and future. His childhood and family links with Prince and Ruby have, in spite of everything, shaped his destiny. His actions, however absurd, do change the world—he finds an impossible hole in the sun, gathers seven impossible tons of Illyrion, and alters the galactic balance of power. As gamesman, Lorq cultivates paradox, only to learn that to ride the edge of chaos may lead to order as well. All events in the novel are marked by such shifts. In the Tarot scene, it is especially clear that action exists on a level other than that of contending wills. Drama here is a process—regulated metamorphoses, sets of three in displacement. Between past and future—tradition and prediction—Lorq holds the contradictory center: "As humor translated to agony, so concern appeared a grin." As Katin tells us, forty-five centuries of human history are mirrored in the symbols and "mythological images" of the Tarot cards. And yet Mouse the Gypsy, whose people bequeathed these cards to humanity, denies they can predict. Time and Ashton Clark have turned things topsy-turvy: once sexually-free nomads have become socketless "eunuchs," guardians of myth skeptics. And it is the enlightened intellectual who now defends occult tradition. In spite of these displacements, residues of the old abide. Mouse's disbelief is colored by irrational fears—he hides cards, disrupts their patterns before the reading is completed. Katin's "faith" is leavened with mockery—he displays annoying erudition, makes flippant jokes ("do not pass go").

At the center of this ambiguous shifting between past and present, fable or truth, Tyy the fortune teller reads her cards, but is unable to interpret them. Myth is suspended in the pure possibility of this uninterpreted present—right where Lorq wants it. All patterns seem to dissolve in inconclusiveness. And yet, at this ominous heart of mystery, a human one suddenly forms: "Lorq took Tyy's arm as she stood. Three expressions struck her face, one after the other: surprise, fear, and the third was when she recognized his." We have again a linear series whose third term is equivocation—instability in balance.

Out of this interplay of trinary patterns a central one emerges—Lorq, Prince, the Sun. This, the core of *Nova*'s epic drama, is more than ever a nexus of ambiguity and potentiality. The cards say a young man will come between Lorq and his flaming sun. Indeed, Mouse has hidden an important card in his game—the *Sun* (he later gives it back, but what does this avail when to have a card—in this game—is at the same time to cut it from one's future?). Depicted on this card are two boys—one dark, one light—holding hands: one looks at the sun, the other at the shadows they cast. Lorq reads this microcosm in terms of agonic struggle—the boys' hands are locked for a fight, here is "the clash of all opposites under the sun." But how opposite are they? If Lorq sees Prince and himself, Mouse asks which is which? Both antagonists apparently have like backgrounds: Prince has blue eyes and black hair, Lorq Negro and Nordic ancestors. If this is to be Cain and Abel, then both brothers bear the mark, the curse. Prince cherishes his artificial hand (because of it he is "missing a socket"), Lorq does the same with the scar that Prince inflicts—he could easily have it removed. The presence of an Idas and Lynceos (again black and white twins, but unbalanced without their third brother) makes us think of the Dioscuri—the "heavenly twins," *Fratres Helenae*, immortal Pollux and mortal Castor. But once again, which is which? Prince seems unkillable: after Lorq's attack he is resurrected, but as a corpse-like monster in liquid suspension. And if Lorq finally kills him, it is only to fly his paradoxical *Black Cockatoo* through the heart of the sun to a living death in blindness. What is more, each is alike in his strange passion for Ruby. Her love for each in turn creates a violently incestuous triangle of passion that closes in the "kiss of death"—the hollow poisoned tooth she prepares for Lorq but doesn't use. At their final meeting, when she tells him of this weapon, he courts it in suicidal fashion, forcing her to kiss him. What he brings about instead is an even more grotesque *liebestod*: Prince shatters his life-sustaining tank with his artifical hand, Ruby kills herself by kissing his drug-covered "corpse." Lorq's suicidal plunge into the nova is the culmination of this bizarre triple love-death. As he gathers his improbable element with mechanical hands, he sees in these fragments the ruins of Ruby's face. This card represents the dynamic system that informs the action in *Nova*—man at the intersection of time and perfection, lawlessness at the heart of balance.

There is a fearful symmetry to the endless metamorphoses in this novel. The *Cockatoo* sinks, the *Roc* rises. Lorq attains balance only in destruction, wholeness only in dissolution. Mouse and Katin bring order only because they have looked on chaos. With Lorq they form a compensating triad. Like him they too appear to be divided beings. Mouse's lack of voice (the minstrel who cannot sing) seems the result of some deep split in his being: "Even if the physical difficulty is corrected there are no nerve connections within the brain to manipulate the physically corrected part." At the heart of each system is man, at his center this mannikin—a small nerve cluster that "looks more or less like a template of a human being." Among this receding series of doubles, each element is irrevocably separated, bearing no relation to the other. This profound rupture is perhaps "what's wrong with Prince's arm," or with Lorq's scar—the moral and physical nevertheless intersect at this point of chaos. Here is another set of "semi-precious stones." In all of Delany's novels these remain separate, yet in some way are "braided" together. This can trap man—it did so with Vol's serpentine line, it will do so again when the nameless hero of *Dhalgren* wraps himself in his enigmatic chain of prisms. Or man can (as in this trio of novels)be braider of his own divided existence. By the fact of his quest alone Lobey connects worlds. The new triad that forms in *Nova*—Lorq, Mouse, Katin—not only brings unity out of disorder, but raises this act of reconstruction to a level of conscious will.

Again division seems the precondition for new order. Like Lorq, Mouse apparently cultivates his divided existence: he walks with one boot, one bare foot. The stigma accepted, worn openly, leads to construction: when Mouse vows allegiance to Lorq as master, he does so by placing his bare foot on Lorq's booted one. As usual, there is a destructive counterthrust: Mouse intersects with Lorq's fateful love triangle by doubling his master's aggression—Lorq blasts Prince with the sensory syrynx, Mouse Ruby. But if this syrynx itself is a divided entity, its primary function is artistic. The destruction of Prince and Ruby brings about a corresponding restructuring on the plane of art. In this alternate triangle the apex shifts to Katin. He likewise is a split being—the tall man who loves small moons. But moons have planets; as Lorq's satellite, he receives the reflected light of his captain's fall into the nova. The light he gets, however, is a new vision—as man and artist. His fixation on the past is mirrored by an artistic "limp"—his pursuit of the "archaic" novel form. But Mouse, too, as artist, is equally crippled. Without a voice (words to music), the improviser is just as surely isolated—this time in the sensual present. Lorq the iconoclast, reaching for the future,ironically proceeds over a circular trail marked by the same stone dragons—from New Brazillia via his aunt's Alkane Institute and back. This enigmatic image of cultures irremediably separated in time ties together Lorq's chaotic life like a chain or bracelet. It takes his quest to the past to thrust his two companions into the future. The Alkane Institute gives way in the end to Alkane—New Brazillia's moon. From this vantage point Katin will write his novel—a broken chain of words that paradoxically is whole. Katin doubles Lorq in his plunge into the sun, only to emerge as man and artist reawakened to the sensuous now: "I realized how much I hadn't looked at. . . . " And in making Mouse the subject of his novel, this immediate present will be preserved for the future. What is more, in the very act of writing it, Katin defies the jinx of the past: "Remember all those writers who died before they finished their Grail recountings?. . . The only way to protect myself from the jinx, I guess, would be to abandon it before I finish the last"—so the novel ends. The fatal chain is both broken and closed, the narrative both open-ended and circular—*if* the novel we have in our hands is Katin's.

In its cultivation of paradoxes *Nova* is highly stylized, to the point almost of preciosity. Yet somehow the adventure story carries it—we experience love, violence, memorable actions. If these two lives balance, it is in a particular way. In developing his tale, Delany has inverted the traditional epic relationship, in which the human subject (the quest) dominates the "form." Here instead is a "subjunctive epic." Men do not struggle against an inhuman system so much as *inside* an unhuman one. At the extreme limits of patterns indifferent to human values this human "content" is re-introduced and heroic actions re-examined in a context that frees them from the anthropocentrism of views such as "glory" or "absurdity." Everywhere in *Nova* seekers after meaning or meaninglessness pass beyond to encounter the neutral dynamic of change-in-order. Instead of absurdity they find ambiguity; instead of doubt uncertainty. "There is a death whose only meaning is that it was died to defend chaos," says Lorq. Yet in this labyrinth of verbal system he neither dies nor alters the triadic order of things: he strikes down one third of the cosmos, another rises, the third "goes staggering." In proclaiming Lorq as Lord and Illyrion as goal, he names only emptiness—a hollow man in a hollow sun. Katin too has difficulty naming himself: "I think. . . therefore I. . . I am Katin Crawford?" But can the artist control any more than the man of action? Is this the beginning of Cartesian reconstruction, or solipsism ("He was the thought. There was no place in here to anchor")? In like manner the final union of the novel closes on the language form that epitomizes ambiguity—the pun, Katin-Mouse. Everything in this narrative occurs on the subjunctive level. If man is placed at the center of systems, he is haunted by the possibility that relation between the two (homological or causal) is lacking. Katin wonders if a focus on the present "might" give his projected narrative more "momentum." Indeed, in *Nova* it is beyond all loss of meaning that captain and crew act out the patterns of epic quest, and thus restore to them (in this world turned inside-out) a strange "Goedelian" solidity and texture. Mouse's syrynx is a much more fearful weapon than Lobey's "ax"; Sebastian's "dark pets" actually save Lorq from Ruby's nets. Idas and Lynceos choose to stay with Lorq though his quest will send their world staggering; Mouse will help Lorq win his sun; Katin the contemplative chooses action, taking the plunge alongside his captain. What gives *Nova* its strength is this reaffirmation at the indifferent heart of system of collective human action—not isolated (as with Rydra and Butcher) in the arena of the mind, but bursting into the cosmic one of life and death.

FROM THE TIDES OF LUST TO TRITON: OLD PATTERNS, NEW DIRECTIONS

The complexities and perplexities of Delany's latest novels—*The Tides of Lust* (1973), *Dhalgren* (1975) and *Triton* (1976)—are too much to discuss in the space remaining—another study is needed for that. The directions they take, however, can be plotted. It is perhaps best to say that these works are not inferior to those of the *Nova* cycle, but rather (as Delany might say) "different." Yet even that must be said with reserve, for the patterned dynamics of threes and twos, the intricacies of palimpsest and filagree exposed in the earlier novels are repeated here, complicated in fact to a degree many find intolerable. The question to ask, with a writer of this sophistication, is why these complications, to what end? New themes and orientations that first appear in some of the transitional short stories collected in *Driftglass* (1971) are developed here—sex, the shrinking of focus from wide-flung galaxies to the here and now, Southern or urban violence in modern America. The Black Captain in *Tides* compares boats between ports and ships between stars—the novel is an "adventure into the sexual unknown." *Dhalgren* transfers the strangeness of the stars to a surreal urban landscape—the realm of "realistic" fiction suddenly becomes the unknown. If Kamp the astronaut cannot describe the moon—it has no referent, is "different"—over Bellona two moons and a giant red sun inexplicably rise. *Triton* returns to the conventional space of SF, but the focus remains "realistic"—here as in *Dhalgren* the landscape is a mental one. These novels investigate less man's relation to linguistic or natural systems than the role he plays as maker of chaos at the heart of a human or social system. Increasingly, Delany places shadowy, uninteresting, dubious beings at the center. The hero of *Dhalgren* projects chaos; as artist, however, he cannot order it—Kid's "notebook" (which may not even be his) is no more than the mirror of moral fragmentation. *Triton* places us more squarely at a moral intersection. Bron Hellstrom is an artist only insofar as he elaborates his rationalizations and equivocations. Lobey was confused by others in a world rebuilding. Bron's world, on the contrary, is deconstructing all around him—what he builds up instead is a web of lies and moral subterfuge. Even more, *Triton* stands at the antipodes of a work like *Nova*. Where Lorq faces the perils of heroic choice, Bron lives the cowardice of moral choice. The problem of moral responsibility is simply surpassed by Lorq's metaphysical quest to the core of mythical and natural systems. For Bron, however, in the inner unheroic world of the self-examining mind, the maze remains one essentially of moral possibility. Restated, paradoxically, in Delany's "structuralist" novel—with its unhuman dynamics in which men ultimately "function" rather than act—is the question of moral responsibility. Bron's mind mirrors (but to what extent does it generate, or is it responsible for) the social system around him?

In both *Einstein* and *Nova* the realm of action is one of crime and chaos. The compensating order is brought about by art. In these novels the intersection remains the questing hero—Lobey narrates, Lorq's example drives his companions to "speak out of the net." The protagonists of *Tides* and *Dhalgren*, however, as artists or examples, are powerless to restore order. In *Tides* traditional moral opposites, Faust and the Devil, become artist-doubles, alike in their inability to create an artistic whole: on one hand there is the primitive "log" of the Captain, on the other the decadent Proctor "doomed to restoring old work with the energy I want to put toward new." Yet the novel itself, structured from without, is elaborately circular. The ordering of triple themes (sex, time and art) is as artificial and precious as Proctor's emblematic painted clock: "A square clock had been painted, in *grisaille*, with four human orifices, two male and two female, at noon, three, six, and nine. The long hand was a penis, the short, a hirsute sack: they swung round the day." This time the stones on the string are sexual perversion, violence, rape, murder of innocents. The artist remains unconcerned with morality—symmetry comes first. This novel places us not at an intersection but at a split. On a far vaster scale, *Dhalgren* does the same. Its hero is neither hero nor artist; he is unable to act or create. As protagonist in search of his name, his maze is verbal and mythical (Kidd, the Kid,

Apollo and Daphne, Newboy the poet, new boy in town, Grendalgren. . .). Primarily, however, his labyrinth is moral: the landscape he wanders through is made of the scattered and shifting fragments of one life. Again, we have a highly patterned work, simultaneously circular (the final line joins the first) and linear (in spite of the welter of "overlays" the story reads in a straight line). But this form is imposed from without—within there is 900 pages of chaos, the novel as notebook, mirror of a world that is itself the projection of the hero's moral confusion. The burning city is also utopia (everything is free), racial and sexual union is structured but meaningless in terms of values, violence is inconsequential (rape becomes a pun, Moon in June). Kid enters and retreats; aesthetic balance does not bring us to pass moral judgment but to suspend it. This novel with its "brass orchids" (a poem and a weapon) is Delany's ultimate garland of flowers of evil.

Triton is more problematical—as such it clearly marks a new direction, perhaps (as with *Towers*) a retreat from preciosity toward the human and tragic implications of man-in-the-system. If so, it turns *Nova* inside out. There, as man confronts systems he didn't make, heroic vanity and collective action (by sympathy if nothing else) take on positive moral value. If *Triton* pits a man against his systems, however, it does so from inside—the struggler against nets becomes more than ever their weaver. Mouse's extinct voice raised the question of man's physical congruity with his encompassing systems. With Bron we have a moral cripple wandering in the maze of psychological possibility: to what extent has such a "flaw" generated the "heterotopia" that encloses him? The world of *Triton* is an "overdetermined system" where absolute mobility is paradoxically absolute isolation, and freedom "hegemony." As logical systems become personal property, they compartmentalize: "By definition my problem is insoluble." Theater plays for an audience of one. The chains of non-related entities thus generated tend entropically toward chaos: the "ninety-seven sayable mantras/mumbles," Bron's twenty-two digit government identity number, the simple sentences dismembered into "modular relationships." Across this landscape Bron is apparently seeking to identify himself in terms of certain "values"—society, heroism, love. But his choices, we discover, are not between real entities (personal malice or passion no longer seem to exist " out there"), but between logical alternatives, coded responses, "literary" models—one chapter is entitled "*La geste d'Hellstrom*," the other "Idylls in Outer Mongolia." In this sense Bron is the existentialist hero keyed one degree higher—not parodied so much as anatomized. His freedom is not dreadful but inconsequential.

At the same time, however, Bron is anti-hero. The paths he takes lead him at all moments to the edge of a new moral intersection. In "metalogics" he hovers on the point of "slippage" between connotation and denotation, real space and "significant space." The sex changes are a similar slippage: the triad of Sam, Bron, the Spike is an infernal *chasser-croiser* whose presiding spirit is not the androgyne but the man-fish monster of the title. Overriding these is a "moral slippage." Announced in *Tides*, anticipated in *Dhalgren* when Lanya reverts to selling sex in a world that has no need for money, this process controls Bron's actions. Both freedom and moral responsibility would seem meaningless in a world where man functions as part of any system of chaos and order. The system of this new novel, though, could be that outlined in the Valery quote that heads a chapter in *Tides*: "I leave you free to choose whatever lie you think worthiest to be the truth." Bron chooses the lie. If he is an artist at all, it is of prevarication—rationalizing his own insignificant experience into epics, converting dubious motives into shining intentions and values. Ironically, some things in *Triton* are simpler and more direct: "Ordinary, informal, nonrigorous language overcomes all these problems." The webs Bron weaves not only blind him to reality (Spike was and is a man) but push off any real relationships offered (Audri). "Slippage" here is a neutral process; but it is also moral backsliding—and Bron is clearly judged. If his world collapses (outer and inner, war and mind), it is because (it is implied) he lived the lie.

The recent Delany himself seems a Triton. On one hand he pursues his arduous career as theoretician of SF—expanding the domain of his chosen genre by claiming it the modern mode of fiction *par excellence*, the one most suited to deal with the complexities of paradox and probability, chaos, irrationality, and the need for logic and order. On the other he has, in his latest novel, returned creation on the level of system to conventional SF space, and in doing so raised the problem of returning man as moral center of an overwrought universe. It is this split that runs through our "literature of exhaustion" in general. Let us hope that here, at this intersection of descriptive system and moral judgment, there will be fusion, some new form of dynamic creation.

BIOGRAPHY AND BIBLIOGRAPHY

SAMUEL RAY DELANY JR. was born April 1, 1942, in New York, New York. After attending several schools for the mentally gifted, Delany made his first professional sale (a nonfiction piece) to *Seventeen* in 1960; his first novel was published in 1962. Delany has won four Nebula Awards, including two for best novel of the year, for *Babel-17* and *The Einstein Intersection*; he also received a Hugo Award for his short story, "Time Considered As a Helix of Semi-Precious Stones." With his wife, the well-known poet Marilyn Hacker, and a young daughter, Delany divides his time between New York, San Francisco, and London, England.

1. *The Jewels of Aptor*. Ace, New York, 1962, 156p, Paper, Novel
2. *Captives of the Flame*. Ace, New York, 1963, 147p, Paper, Novel

2A. reprinted as: *Out of the Dead City*. Sphere, London, 1968, 143p, paper, Novel

3. *The Towers of Toron*. Ace, New York, 1964, 140p, Paper, Novel
4. *City of a Thousand Suns*. Ace, New York, 1965, 156p, Paper, Novel
5. *The Ballad of Beta-2*. Ace, New York, 1965, 96p, Paper, Novel
6. *Empire Star*. Ace, New York, 1966, 102p, Paper, Novel
7. *Babel-17*. Ace, New York, 1966, 173p, Paper, Novel
8. *The Einstein Intersection*. Ace, New York, 1967, 142p, Paper, Novel
9. *Nova*. Doubleday, Garden City, 1968, 279p, Cloth, Novel
10. *The Fall of the Towers* [includes *Captives of the Flame*, *The Towers of Toron*, and *City of a Thousand Suns*]. Ace, New York, 1970, 413p, Paper, Coll.
11. *Driftglass*. Nelson Doubleday, Garden City, 1971, 274p, Cloth, Coll.
12. *The Tides of Lust*. Lancer, New York, 1973, 173p, Paper, Novel
13. *Dhalgren*. Bantam, New York, 1975, 880p, Paper, Novel
14. *Triton*. Bantam, New York, 1976, 370p, Paper, Novel

15-18. Delany also edited four volumes in the *Quark* paperback magazine series with his wife Marilyn Hacker (1970-1971).